MW00683171

UNLOCKING

UNIVERSITY OF CALGARY
Press

UNLOCKING

AMY LEBLANC

Brave & Brilliant Series
ISSN 2371-7238 (Print) ISSN 2371-7246 (Online)

© 2021 Amy LeBlanc
All rights reserved

University of Calgary Press
2500 University Drive NW
Calgary, Alberta
Canada T2N 1N4
press.ucalgary.ca

No part of this book may be reproduced in any format whatsoever without prior written permission from the publisher, except for brief excerpts quoted in scholarship or review.

This is a work of fiction. Names, characters, businesses, places, events and incidents are either the products of the author's imagination or used in a fictitious manner. Any resemblance to actual persons, living or dead, or actual events is purely coincidental.

LIBRARY AND ARCHIVES CANADA CATALOGUING IN PUBLICATION

Title: Unlocking / Amy LeBlanc.
Names: LeBlanc, Amy, 1995- author.
Series: Brave & brilliant series ; no. 19. 2371-7238
Description: Series statement: Brave & brilliant series, 2371-7238 ; 19
Identifiers: Canadiana (print) 20210124326 | Canadiana (ebook) 20210124350 | ISBN 9781773851396 (softcover) | ISBN 9781773851402 (PDF) | ISBN 9781773851419 (EPUB) | ISBN 9781773851426 (Kindle)
Classification: LCC PS8623.E323 U55 2021 | DDC C813/.6—dc23

The University of Calgary Press acknowledges the support of the Government of Alberta through the Alberta Media Fund for our publications. We acknowledge the financial support of the Government of Canada. We acknowledge the financial support of the Canada Council for the Arts for our publishing program.

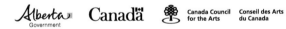

Printed and bound in Canada by Marquis Book Printing
♻ This book is printed on 70lb Opaque Smooth Cream paper

Editing by Aritha van Herk
Copyediting by Naomi K. Lewis
Cover image: Colourbox 15913426
Chapter break image: Colourbox 2057738
Cover design, page design, and typesetting by Melina Cusano

Keyed In

Consider this key I keep on my key chain.
I can't remember what door it opened.
I can't discard the key.

Maybe it opened the door to the cupboard
in which I kept my life story.
Where did that cupboard get to?

Maybe it fit the door of that old Chev
I drove away in when I left home.
Why didn't I keep a key to the house?

But maybe it is a key to the house.
Too bad the house is gone.
It's still the place where I live.

—Robert Kroetsch

Euphemia's Prologue

Three can keep a secret if two of them are dead. Who was it that said that?

I suppose it doesn't matter (since the one who said it is most likely the first to go). Here's what I've always said: a goldfish will eventually grow to fit the size of its bowl, and the same is true of secrets. In a confined space, a secret will expand to be as large as the space itself. When the boundaries of the space change, so do the dimensions of the secret. It's basic—when a secret is patiently fed, it begins to grow. An impatient gardener will water too much, fertilize at the wrong time, and pluck their turnips from the soil when they could have grown, with a little patience, twice as bulbous.

In Snowton, Alberta, a secret that began as small as a seed was fed until it flourished like a crocus in spring.

That isn't to say there was a shortage of secrets before the latest one. Alexander Davy's parents locked him in a toolshed when he wet the bed as a child. Once, while they were planning a bingo fundraiser for repairs to the town library, Alexander was in the shed for forty-six hours. Mr. Davy was practising how he might call bingo numbers—*Seventeen, Dancing Queen. Sixty-one, Bakers Bun. Eighty-five, Staying Alive*—while Alexander pulled his last lint-covered piece of gum from his pants pocket to moisten his mouth. I was with Mr. Davy, Alexander's father, when he passed away years after the incident in the shed. He told me that he had only ever wanted to make the boy *strong*, but I never understood what he meant by that. A clematis cannot grow without a trellis to lean on for support.

Mr. Davy himself had been bullied as a child, and he wanted something different for Alexander (who was not present when his father died—he was dealing cards at a casino in Vancouver at the time).

Here's another secret: as teenagers, Ben Higgins, Mark Dull, and Edward Till spray-painted *Indigo Vince is a slut* on the outside wall of the bowling alley where Indigo used to work to support her mother's drug habit. I only found out because Indigo came to my house for a handful of the polypore pieces I nurtured in my backyard. Generally speaking, most polypores are harmless, but she wanted polypores of the genus *Hapalopilus*, a species that can cause kidney failure, which leads to fluid retention, confusion, weakness, coma, etcetera, etcetera. Indigo thought she might slip some into their soft drinks the next time they came to the bowling alley. I gave it to her, but as far as I know, she never went through with it. A part of me wishes that she had. It would have made for a more interesting year.

Even now, Wanda Alpin talks in her sleep and tells her husband that she wants a divorce, but then wakes up with no recollection of having said anything of the sort. Her husband came to me and asked if any of my plants could help her sleep more soundly. It seems that being dumped night after night was beginning to take its toll. I gave him some valerian root to boil with chamomile and suggested he add a tablespoon of honey for sweetness. He never returned for more, so I assume the mixture worked. If it didn't, he may have finally learned how to cope with rejection.

Angela Cullen stole three thousand dollars from the fund for flood relief in 2013. The town council had stapled a milk jug to the telephone pole outside the library to collect donations. Angela was in charge of emptying the jug each night and tallying the donations, but she only wrote down half of the actual amount. The rest went into empty peanut butter jars in her basement. I can't find any reason for that theft other than blatant greed, and I certainly don't blame her for that.

I keep all of these secrets like seedlings in my hands. The leaves on my poplar tree have begun turning inside out, and a creeping bellflower has spread itself into the sidewalk cracks in front of my house. The rabbits munch on the blooms and leaves. Regardless, the flower persists and grows. If you try to pluck a creeping bellflower from the earth, you will discover that its roots travel under lawns and fences and even beneath concrete, like a nervous system. Invasive and stubborn, these plants thrive in all conditions.

I am alone most of the time, and I speak to my plants to help them grow. Whoever said classical music helps plants germinate and ripen has never spoken to me. My vines wither if I play Mozart, but twist and grasp and climb when I speak to them. I tell them secrets, which they absorb like nutrients from the soil. The earth of this town is ripe with whispers and furtive conversations. The key to understanding is to soak everything in like a bearded iris and try not to let the secrets turn to rot.

I have been skirting around the periphery of Louise Till's secret for some time. I have seen her taking notes as secretary in town council meetings. I see how she separates herself from what she writes. But you don't take on a role like that unless you're at least a little curious about the lives of others. By watching Lou, I have learned that the part of a key that enters a lock is called the blade. What we hold as we slide a key into a lock is the bow. The shoulder is what keeps a key from getting swallowed in the jaws of a lock. The deepest part of a key's cut is called the valley. The reason my key works at my house and yours does not is that they have different codes, individual delineations that dictate what a key can be used for. A key's valley, shoulder, code, and other features make up the small piece of metal we use for security. A sense of security, anyway.

I have been observant and patient, as any good gardener should be, but I can sense that the contours of Louise's secret are about to change.

Lou's Story: First Winter

CHAPTER 1

Lou brushed snow from the sides of sloping headstones and jangled the keys on her chain. She knew that the earth was always shifting, tectonic plates were moving, earthquakes, hurricanes, floods, and volcanoes erupted and shook and submerged.

On a level that Lou could witness, the cemetery had gradually begun to slope toward the east. The ground had only begun to shift visibly in recent years, but the headstones had an unmistakable tilt to the left, which meant they had been nudging athwart for some time, and most had begun to bump sides with their neighbours. As she looked at her parents' headstones, their carved edges barely touching, she thought that perhaps this is how tectonics persist: one infinitesimally small shift in the earth and everything tilts out of balance.

She took a few minutes and counted the keys in her hands—*forty-two*—she counted them again—*forty-two*—which meant that she had one hundred and sixty-six locked safely away in the store. In her whole collection, she had twelve patterned keys, ninety-nine identical Weiser keys, Schlage keys of various vintages, three latchkeys, and a number of generic keys that looked almost identical. To the untrained eye, the minute variances between keys are indistinguishable, but Lou was aware of the unique tactility of each and its corresponding house in town.

She had been collecting others' keys for the past year and had surprised herself with her seamless ability to lie and deceive in order to attain them. She'd imagined fibsters and spinners of yarns as men with ascots and spats, or women in fake fur coats with cigarette holders in their gloved hands. She never questioned that her perception of liars seemed to be rooted in 1920s imagery, and she never imagined that she, of all people, would keep a secret of this magnitude. And lie about it so adroitly.

After her father's death, she'd inherited his hardware store. When she worked there as a girl, her father used to smooth down her hair to place padded earmuffs on her head before he turned on the key cutter. He guided her gloved hands through the cuts and notches as if metal were no more difficult to cut than butter. Her mother compared the sound of the key cutter to a cat being castrated, but Lou never disliked the sound. She associated it with the controlled pressure of her fingertips against the wing nuts and thumb turns and the smell of her father's cologne. Her favourite part came after the key was cut, and she could hold its edges against the deburring wheel to smooth any roughness away. This was when she felt most involved in the process. She didn't have a machine making cuts for her; she could hold the key against the wheel and feel its harshness filed away bit by bit. If she went too far, she'd need to cut the key again. It was a balance, she found, of firmness and caution.

But now she felt incautious. She hadn't planned to keep anyone's keys, and she'd been blindsided by her own compulsion to do just that.

After she inherited the store, her first customer was Frank Blake. He had a new partner and needed Lou to cut a copy of his housekey. Lou told him to come back in thirty minutes, as she was finishing another project, but she guaranteed that the new key would be ready upon his return. Lou didn't have a plan or even an inkling of what she might do with Frank's key; she just needed to keep it. And to keep it secret. When he came back, he picked up his keys, paid, and left, with never any reason to suspect that she had buried a second copy in the storeroom filing cabinet beneath ancient bank statements. Her mother had kept each paper bank statement over the years (she'd refused to move to online delivery), because she felt that they might be useful someday. In hindsight, Lou could see that her mother was preparing her to take over the store, gathering snippets of information that Lou might need when she was on her own. In this way, Lou thought of her mother like a magpie. She gathered what was needed, kept it safe, and made a home out of a nest filled with string and sawdust.

In the cemetery, she tightened her scarf around her throat and breathed in the smell of her well-worn clothing as the wind rolled through town and in between listing headstones. The scarf had been her mother's, but it hadn't smelled like her for a long time. She often thought of her parents and what they might say if they could see her, her pockets full of other people's keys. Lou closed her eyes and heard a whisper but was fairly certain that she had been the one to speak. Sometimes, she was taken off guard by the sound of her own voice. There were days when she didn't speak to anyone until a customer came into the store. She was usually surprised by the clarity of her own voice; the one she heard in her head was gravelly, more like her mother's. Nonetheless, she imagined that the wind carried her mother's voice towards her: *I've got the key to my castle in the air, but whether I can unlock the door remains to be seen.* She liked to remind herself that the cemetery would be here, braced against the wind, far longer than she would. These dusty headstones weren't going anywhere anytime soon.

Lou walked the perimeter of the cemetery twice each morning. Between eight and eight-thirty, a group of men mummified from head to toe in spandex and elastic ran around its perimeter.

Hi Lou.
Morning
Hey.
Hi.

Hi Lou.
Skip to my Lou!
How are you doing, Lou?

They each tossed a breathless greeting towards her as they flew past, pumping their arms in time with their legs, fleece headbands covering their ears against the winter chill. The last greeting came from Bart Hastings, a local writer and the most recent addition to the group, who told her that he'd taken up running to keep his creativity focused and consistent, and to counteract the sedentary nature of his work. She didn't know him well—she had cut keys for him only once—but she knew he wrote mystery novels that occasionally bore a resemblance to events and people in town. No one took issue with this. They all expected that someday he might be the town's claim to fame. Snowton couldn't compete with the Torrington Gopher Hole Museum, where tourists could see stuffed gophers in wedding dresses or gopher facsimiles of early Alberta settlers. Lou had never understood the appeal of the gopher museum, but she had spent many afternoons there with her children and her husband.

She'd see the runners (she'd named them 'the chums') at varying times of the day and in different locations. Sometimes they were jogging, other times they did long, slow variations on lunges across fields, or squats where their backsides almost touched the snowy earth, but they were in a constant state of motion. She often wondered if they ever stopped to eat or drink a cup of coffee together. Her father had never been a runner, but he used to step outside the hardware store to chat when they ran by. He'd stand still, and the 'chums' would run in place—and her father seemed to belong with them, somehow. He'd invite them into the store for coffee, which they politely refused, and they'd go on their way. Lou still kept the pot of coffee on and drank four to five cups of high-test each day, but her eyes twitched only occasionally, and her heart fluttered with nerves whether she was caffeinated or not. She would try to kick the habit soon; it was just a matter of how soon.

She stepped between the cremation-urn garden and the in-ground burial plots to pluck a few dandelions that grew around headstones and had somehow survived the first round of winter even though the odds were stacked against them. Weeds, she thought, were always poking through the soil. Nothing could destroy them. She remembered reading that a woman's mourning clothes used to be called Widow's Weeds. She wasn't a widow, but she didn't know what to call herself (Adult Orphan? Remainder? Undone?).

She wiped off mud that caked across familiar names. The cemetery housed only one hundred and fifty plots; many of the people from town who died were buried a short drive away in Calgary, because their children and grandchildren had left town years before. But everyone who had ever mattered to Lou was buried here: her grandparents, her aunts and uncles, her old friends, her first baby, and, finally, her parents, buried in a row overlooking the stream and surrounded by evergreens. The slant of the cemetery ground somehow made the spot more inviting. There was a wrought iron fence that surrounded the graveyard, and one of the latches on the gate had been broken for as long as Lou could remember. There was no shortage of townsfolk who could have fixed it, but it had become a fixture of the Snowton Cemetery's mythology. No one knew where the stories began, but according to legend, the broken latch allowed the spirits of the Snowton Cemetery to wander the town at night, peeking into their old houses, checking up on their loved ones. For the younger citizens, this legend worked to keep them out of the cemetery after dark, for fear of encountering the undead. For the older citizens, it gave them something akin to equanimity. The cemetery was a silent space, but it was a place Lou felt she could belong to, because it was imperfect. She could come to the cemetery with unwashed hair, holes in her socks, and a cluttered mind.

She'd wanted to bring the twins with her to visit their grandparents' graves, but her children were uneasy about cemeteries. Even at sixteen, they hadn't outgrown the tendency to believe that everything about death was frightening. When their cat had died with fluid in his lungs after drinking water from beneath their front step, her children hadn't wanted to touch him. Lou thought he looked like he was sleeping; she was the one that wrapped him in a pillowcase, placed him in a shoebox, and buried him in the backyard beneath the poplar tree. She didn't pressure her children to go to the cemetery, because as a child she'd been anxious in the same way. She'd remained so until her grandmother's funeral, when her mother explained that cemeteries weren't places of death so much as they were places of rest. After that conversation, Lou began visiting the graves of relatives who had died before she was born. She found herself in a daily routine where she placed a hand on the top of each tombstone and counted to three before moving to the next. Counting quieted her mind, and the palpability of the headstones gave her something concrete to focus on.

The cemetery was one of the few places where she could shut her mind off for minutes at a time. She counted the headstones and the evergreens that surrounded her; she picked pinecones off the path and placed them beneath the trees. She'd arrive at her parents' graves with plucked dandelions in her gloved hands, but often bouquets of dahlias and forget-me-nots had already been laid on the grass. She knew that her parents had been well-loved, and that should have made the grief easier to bear, but somehow it added to sorrow's desolation. She was never sure why, but her grief took the shape of a yellow clay pot that sat in her body just behind her stomach. When grief overflowed, it poured black over the edges of the pot. When it subsided for moments, the clay pot emptied, and she could see yellow again. When she thought about community grief, the pot overflowed more quickly than she could imagine, an outpouring.

On this particular morning, she sat down between the headstones and felt the pressure of the stones touch her shoulder blades on both sides. Lou ran her right thumb and middle finger around the space where her wedding ring used to be. She had told Edward that the ring was missing; she said it must have slipped off when she was out, since the ring was too large for her shrinking finger. She had lost weight in the last year, but Louise knew exactly where the wedding ring was, and she had no intention of retrieving it.

Edward came home one day to find Lou on her knees in the garden. She'd been planting lavender, rosemary, dill, and chives, and she'd removed her gardening gloves to work on a particularly tough root with her fingernails. When she finished gardening, she discovered that her ring was neither on her finger nor in the glove; she decided to leave it in the dirt. She read a newspaper article about a woman whose wedding ring had been lost in her garden. She found the ring thirteen years later when she harvested her new crop of vegetables and found the ring in the center of a misshapen carrot. The carrot had grown out from the ring so that it looked like a cinched waist. This woman had left her husband years before the ring was found.

Seated in the grass, Lou brushed cat hair from the edges of her sleeves, and she began to speak:

Hi Mom. Hi Dad.

She always paused to give time for a response.

No, I'm doing well. Really, I am. The kids are healthy, Edward is healthy. Molly's decided that she wants to be an engineer, so we're researching universities for her. Stewart still isn't sure what he wants to do, but he'll get there eventually.

Lou brushed her hair away from her eyes.

The store is fine, Dad. Remember the router you wanted that was on backorder? It finally arrived, so I can finish the edging on that hobby horse. Yes, I will, I promise.

She traced the edge of his headstone.

All right, I'll see you both tomorrow.

Lou stood up too fast and was struck with sudden lightheadedness. She'd never run out of words to say so quickly, and she hadn't even said what she'd intended to. She knew they couldn't hear her, but she needed to get certain words out of her head and into the air, and she'd failed to say them. Everyone else knew that she and Edward were separating, but her parents hadn't been told. It reminded her of folklore she'd heard about telling the bees; it was a custom that bees should be informed of important events like births, deaths, general comings and goings, funerals, weddings. If the bees weren't told, they would leave the hive and the honey would dry up. The bees were worthy of respect, and that respect came in the form of stories. Her parents weren't going anywhere, she knew that, but they still deserved to be told about important events, especially related to their own daughter.

She hesitated and turned to go, but then returned and placed a hand on her father's headstone, tracing her fingers along the inscription from Dickens: *a very little key will open a heavy door.* Lou scraped the dirt away from the headstone with her bitten and cracked fingernails and pushed onwards.

CHAPTER 2

Carbon Monoxide poisoning.
　　What a shame about your parents, dear.
　　I guess we never really know, do we?
　　But they always seemed so happy.
　　Heartbreaking. Just heartbreaking.
　　Lou received a call from the hospital when her parents were
hours away from breathing their last breaths.

　　When the paramedics spoke to Lou about what they'd
found, they told her that the carbon monoxide detector had
been unscrewed from the wall. Lou told them that her parents
often did this when the batteries were low as a reminder to
change them. They couldn't stand the incessant beeping. The
paramedics told her that the car had been running in the
garage, but Lou knew that her father must have been warming
the car so her mother wouldn't be cold, and then got distracted.
It was a combination of bad luck and forgetfulness that had
resulted in catastrophe. The paramedics seemed to insinuate
that her parents had taken their own lives, but Lou knew that
just couldn't be true.

　　She would have noticed if something were wrong.

　　She'd seen them only days before.

　　She couldn't possibly have missed the signs.

　　Lou was soon reminded of the speed with which bad news
can spread in a small town. She never knew how to respond
to such remarks, except to maintain her fervent belief that the
rumours were not true, and that she had known her parents
better than anyone else.

Lou didn't open the store for the first few weeks. She knew what she would find. A leftover coffee cup her father intended to throw out in the morning. Her mother's lavender hand cream. A note in her father's handwriting: *don't forget to order more screws in 5/8" and 1 ¼"*. A note in her mother's hand that said *I love you*. When she did decide to open the store, she put these mementos in a box beneath the counter. She wanted them close, but not in her line of sight.

She couldn't bear to read their handwriting and know that she would never see a new note again.

CHAPTER 3

In her hardware store, Lou carried some state-of-the-art
tools: full set cordless track-saws, titanium hammers, electric
screwdrivers, and lithium jigsaws, but her customers usually
wanted screws, nails, lightbulbs, or cans of paint. She also
carried odd items like cake mixes, postcards, SPF 60 sunscreen,
nightlights, and an old record player.

The hardware store sat at the centre of Main Street in a
town of three thousand and thirty-nine people. There was
one Tim Hortons (facing impending closure), two pizzerias,
a hospital, one public school, one Catholic school, a liquor
store, a café, a pharmacy, a bookstore, the corner store, five
churches, and Lou's hardware store. Indigo Higgins owned
the local bookstore. She stocked poetry from Western Canada,
Bart Hastings' murder mysteries, and books about birds. It was
a well-known fact that Indigo could name collective nouns
for birds in any situation, and she often created opportunities
to mention an asylum of cuckoos, a museum of waxwings, a
charm of goldfinches, or a pretense of bitterns. Each Christmas
since Lou had married Edward, she had bought him a book
from Indigo's store—usually one of the select few that wasn't
about birds and wasn't authored by Bart Hastings. Lou never
knew what else to get him. This year, they hadn't exchanged
gifts at all.

To the left of Lou's cash till stood a revolving rack of paint
chips organized by colour gradient. She sprayed WD40 on the
hinges every morning, but the rack still squeaked as it spun.
The paints had names that she could hardly read without

laughing: Flamingo's Dream (an awful shade of bubblegum pink), Hugs & Kisses (an odd brown that did not remind her of physical affection), Tornado Season (a deep stormy blue), and Mayonnaise (self-explanatory).

The walls of the store were lined with items shelved from floor to ceiling, mostly small, niche items that she hoped the right customer might someday need. To the right of her cash register, she also kept a display of items that her mother and father had made over the years. Some were fastened to the wall with brackets, others sat on a wooden shelf her father had made for this exact purpose. From her father she kept a guitar stand in the shape of a human hand. It used to sit empty, but since his passing, his guitar was nestled between the fingertips for customers to see. Now, she has added a sign reading *Please Do Not Touch*, because children with jam-covered fingers would try to pluck the strings. There was a red blotch below the mahogany-coloured pick guard. From her mother, she had a wooden map of Canada made with tree bark found in each region. It was a passion project of her mother's, one that allowed her to call on all her relatives and friends across the country to track down localized bark.

For the entirety of Lou's life, the store had smelled of sawdust, terracotta flowerpots, and turpentine. This was where she lived now—on a cot in the back room beside a mini-fridge full of nutrition shakes with extra protein, leftover delivery pizza, and beer. Her cat, Magician, lived in the store with her and seemed to prefer this arrangement to living in the old house; she had plenty of perches and power cords to play with. Even though the door opened multiple times per hour, Magician hadn't yet attempted escape. Most of Lou's customers didn't mind the way that Magician snaked around their ankles while they shopped, but her male customers (who didn't dislike cats as a rule) soon discovered that the cat disliked them. Magician liked to sit on a shelf exactly the height of men's heads and give them a gentle, clawless swat behind the ear when they turned their backs. Magician had done the same to Edward when Lou first moved in with him. Lou had gotten the cat from a rescue shelter, and Magician was now nineteen years old—older than Lou's children, older than her marriage. Lou figured that Magician would keep going at full speed until one day she would fall asleep on a shelf next to the lightbulbs and simply wouldn't wake up. Lou couldn't imagine life without the cat. Magician was her tether.

"Your cat just hit me," her customers would say, eyeing Magician warily and giving her a wider berth.

Lou had been living in the store since Thanksgiving, but she knew her sojourn was temporary, only until she could decide on a permanent place of residence. She still had the keys and the rights to her parents' house, where she grew up, but she hadn't set foot inside since they died. She took great care to make sure none of her customers guessed she was living in the store. She knew she would be inundated with invitations to stay at every house in Snowton, and she couldn't bear the looks of inquisitive pity. She'd heard that grieving usually took three, seven, or eighteen months; she'd also heard that it would never end. At this point in her grieving process, she fully expected the latter.

Remarkably, Christmas had not been as uncomfortable as she'd anticipated, because she did not have to return to the house with Edward. Euphemia Rosenbaum had hosted a Christmas dinner where everyone could meet on neutral territory. She'd also invited a number of people that Lou hadn't expected to see, but assumed would have been alone for the holidays if it weren't for Euphemia's invitation: Phillip Dion, Bart Hastings, Eve and Alfred, Frank Blake, Ben Higgins (Indigo was home with the flu), Edward, and the twins. She had been doubtful that they could all fit into Euphemia's dining room, but with some crafty rearranging of chairs and an extra leaf placed in the oak dining set, each guest had a place to sit and a full plate of food in front of them. Lou suspected that

Euphemia wanted a full house; her best friend and partner in crime, Isabella, had been dead for almost a year. She'd been found face-down in an open copy of *To Kill a Mockingbird*, with a half-drunk mug of tea on the table beside her. The doctors said it was old age, but Euphemia wasn't so sure. In the months since her death, Euphemia had mentioned to Lou that she might get police involved, because she suspected some kind of foul play. Lou assumed it was just how Euphemia processed her grief, but she had yet to let go of the idea. Lou felt that she was in no position to criticize how anyone coped, or didn't cope, with grief.

The twins, Molly and Stewart, seemed to enjoy the dinner well enough, and Lou found herself envying them. They'd always had each other growing up. Lou's first baby had died before the twins were born, and they'd never really experienced loss until their grandparents died. Lou thought they were handling her and Edward's separation as well as could be expected, with all of the grace and dignity that sixteen-year-olds could muster. They weren't angry with her, but they also didn't understand why life couldn't stay the way it had always been: two healthy and loving grandparents, and a mother, a father, and a cat all under the same roof.

CHAPTER 4

The snowflakes were crystalline—the kind that nestle between eyelashes and freeze them together. From the register, Lou watched the snow falling outside. She'd had an exceptional number of sales and returns since Christmas. All of the items that needed to be processed were piling up on the counter beside the register, but Lou didn't have the energy to tackle the pile. Earlier that week, Maya Holmes had come into the store and asked Lou to give her only daughter, Cass, a job for the winter. The family was short on money, and Cass was saving up for university. Lou knew how to manage the store alone and knew that she didn't need an employee, but she looked at the pile of returns that seemed to grow by the hour and told Maya to bring the girl into the store that week. Almost immediately after she agreed to take her on, Lou wondered what she'd been thinking. She would be bringing the girl into her home, where she had copied and stashed more than two hundred of her neighbours' keys. Lou nearly called to cancel the offer, but she decided to wait, and a few days later, the bell above the door chimed, and a blast of cold, dry air coiled in Lou's direction. Cass stood in the doorway, far taller and more grown up than Lou remembered her. Lou had folded her cot so that it fit in the corner of the back room, and she'd tried to hide all other signs that she'd been living in the store.

"Good morning, Mrs. Till. Where should I start?"

Lou took a deep breath and prepared herself for the coming challenge.

"Hello, Cass. Let's sit down and have a chat first, shall we?"

Cass lifted the messenger bag that hung across her body and placed it on the floor near a small pile of sawdust. She didn't wear a winter coat, which Lou couldn't understand in Alberta winters. Instead she wore a blue jean jacket with white fleece trim around the collar. Lou didn't point out that there was a hook beside the door where she could hang her bag instead of leaving it in the sawdust. Cass didn't seem to mind her bag getting dirty.

"Well, what is it that you'd like to do here?"

"I'd like to be useful," Cass said.

"Is there anything you're particularly interested in? Woodworking, home repairs, anything like that? Perhaps after some training you could help me with commissioned pieces."

Cass took a moment to consider, and Lou took stock of her. She had a small forehead hidden by blonde bangs, straight cut, which would have been severe on anyone else, but on Cass they were soft. She also had surprisingly dark eyelashes. She didn't wear makeup, which Lou admired (but wasn't sure why), and the girl seemed to be thinking hard enough that Lou felt she might be taking this job at the store seriously.

"I think I'm interested in home repairs—like plumbing or something."

"All right, I can help a little with that. I'm not a certified plumber, but I do have some experience. In the meantime, I could use help processing returns from the holidays." Cass nodded, and her bangs shifted on her forehead but never seemed to settle in her eyes. Whenever Lou had tried bangs, generally after a breakup or some other large transition in her life, she'd become frustrated with their constant presence in her eyes. She'd end up pulling them back with a headband, which she thought made her forehead look like a hammerhead shark's.

Lou gave Cass control of the returns pile and asked her to generate an itemized list of the returned items. She was pleased to discover that the girl put her headphones on, got to work, and mainly kept to herself. She listened deeply to whatever played through her headphones and the occasional *hmm*-sound left her lips. It was the end of the day by the time Cass finished her list of returned items and had rearranged the stock; she removed her headphones to pack up her things.

Lou was still uneasy about how to keep her secrets safe, but she found that she didn't mind having another person in the store. Lou liked hearing a voice other than her own, and the way that Cass occasionally cleared her throat almost felt like a reminder that they were both still there. Cass was a little older than Lou's children; Lou wondered how Maya felt about her oldest and only daughter leaving home for university. Lou supposed that she had no right to try and keep her children close to home when she was the one who had left.

Cass pulled her messenger bag over her head and placed the strap across her shoulder.

"What are you listening to while you work?" Lou asked her.

"Oh, it's just a podcast."

"About what?"

"The dancing plague of 1518."

Lou had never heard of it, and this failing clearly showed on her face.

"These people couldn't stop dancing in this little town in France. A lot of them danced themselves to death."

"Really?"

"Yeah, it's where the tarantella came from. You know, the music? They thought people had been bitten by poisonous spiders, but it was just flour that had gone fungal, and they were all having seizures."

Lou was unsure of how to respond and then said the first words that came to mind, thinking back to the events that took place at Thanksgiving.

"You should talk to Euphemia Rosenbaum if you're interested in stories like that. She'll tell you all about the time it rained meat in Kentucky."

"Oh, the Great Kentucky Meat Shower? I already know about that one."

Lou took a good look at Cass with her distressed jeans and denim jacket, the 'Canadian Tuxedo' as her mother and father used to say.

"Well, I'll see you tomorrow, Mrs. Till. Have a good evening."

"You too, Cass. Say hello to your mother for me. And please, call me Lou."

Another cold gust of air came in through the door, and Lou realized that the store felt quieter than usual after closing. She locked the door behind Cass, turned the open sign around, and walked to the back room to eat the week-old Christmas stuffing she'd kept in the mini-fridge, but that she now worried might have gone fungal.

Since she'd moved out, she'd been thinking of Euphemia more and more. When Lou lived with Edward, she and Euphemia were neighbors, but had never been particularly close. Euphemia had lived alone all these years with her plants and her books. She was something of a mythical figure in Snowton. She knew everyone's secrets before they had time to grow; and yet, no one knew where she got her information. Lou had always perceived Euphemia's as a lonely life, but now she began to crave that kind of solitude. It was possible that sheer peace and quiet was why Euphemia managed to learn a new language every few months. Lou had been over for tea a few times and had attributed her slight discomfort to the overpowering smell of plants growing inside the house. She remembered a moment with Euphemia many months before she'd even begun seriously thinking of a divorce from Edward. Lou was on her way to Euphemia's powder room when she saw something out of the corner of her eye: a small trail of ants streaming from the corner of the wall. One ant carried a piece of plaster and kept breaking the chain of ants to pick it up when it dropped the piece.

When Lou returned from the washroom, Euphemia was sitting in her armchair with a book in her hands: *Ten Ways to Fall in Love with Your Husband.*

"Just a little something I thought you might be needing." After she handed the book to Lou, she placed more almond cookies on a tray and then sent her home with a roast for dinner and a small plant in a terracotta pot. Lou assumed that Euphemia was lonely, but perhaps Euphemia had been happier than anyone else all these years, and *that* was the discomfort Lou felt in her presence.

Lou had grown up in the hardware store. She knew its smells, its sharp corners, and the spots where the floorboards lifted and creaked, but she had never expected to own and manage it by herself, nor had she planned to live there. It wasn't that she didn't value what her parents had worked for; she just knew that she couldn't possibly replace them. She hadn't even planned to stay in Snowton, but then she met Edward. He was head lifeguard at the community pool, or the local festering hole as he called it, and she'd just begun teaching swimming classes to save money for her move to Calgary. She wanted to be in a city with libraries, and museums, and theatres.

Before Lou was married and had her children, she'd wanted to be a poet. She knew there was no financial security in being a poet, but she hoped she could make enough to support herself with her skills from the hardware store and someday perhaps publish some poems. She had been in Snowton her whole life, and she knew there was only room for one 'real writer' in town. Bart Hastings had staked a claim on that title long ago.

They married when the lifeguard was twenty-four and she was twenty-one and two months pregnant. Edward had no intention of leaving Snowton. When she said yes to his proposal, she knew she would be stuck forever. She'd reconciled with that recognition by the time their wedding day came, but the thought of leaving town had crept up on her at strange times in her life: washing the dishes, changing her babies' diapers, tallying up costs against projected sales while her father was out front talking to customers. She almost left once, when Stewart and Molly were ten months old. She'd packed up their diaper bags and dropped them off at the Higgins' house. They didn't have children of their own, and Ben fawned over the twins whenever he saw them. She told Ben she had a doctor's appointment in town and needed to leave the babies with him for a couple of hours. She didn't tell him that she had a bag in the back of the car with enough clothes for one week, all of her medications, and her passport. She got to the edge of town and parked at the sign that said *You are now leaving Snowton. We hope you visit again soon!*

She did a U-turn, drove back into town, and picked up her babies from Ben Higgins, claiming that her doctor's appointment had been cancelled. Ben didn't bat an eye, and she never told anyone what she'd almost done. She went home and took a long time bathing the twins, reconnecting with their little bodies, scrubbing between their fingers and toes, laughing when they splashed water at each other. She tried to wash away what she'd almost done.

Now that she'd taken over the store, she knew more than ever before that she was never going to leave. She curled up on her cot and drifted off to sleep, breathing in the smells of varnish and sawdust.

CHAPTER 5

The next morning, the bell above the door chimed, and Alfred Crumb, her son's best friend, walked in with a brace on his wrist, carrying pieces of wood that may have once constituted a kitchen chair.

"Morning, Al. What brings you in today?"

"Morning, Mrs. Till." Despite the fact that Al was the same age as her son and had been over at their house every day for more than a decade, he still spoke to her as if they were meeting for the first time. "Mother asked me to bring this in and see if you could fix it. I was trying to change a lightbulb, and the chair snapped underneath me."

"My god, are you all right?"

He waved the brace as if to say *never better*, and in the process of waving, he dropped one of the wooden pieces to the floor.

"Mother loves this chair. She'll be so disappointed if it can't be fixed."

"If too many of the pieces have splintered, there may not be anything to fix, but I'll see what I can do."

He nodded and moved to the side of the store where Lou stocked lightbulbs.

"Mrs. Till, would you mind cutting a copy of our housekey? I lost mine." From his pocket he drew a silver Schlage key that looked all too familiar to Lou. "This one is my mother's."

"Not a problem, give me thirty minutes for the key and a week or two for the chair."

Lou had a copy of their housekey in the back storeroom, but she couldn't give it to him without providing an explanation.

"Thank you, Mrs. Till. I appreciate it."

Goosebumps crept up her arms the second time Al called her that. Mrs. Till was and would always be her mother-in-law.

She took the key from his outstretched hand and placed it on top of her 045 HD Performance Series cutting machine.

CHAPTER 6

On New Year's Eve, Lou's seventy-sixth day of living in the store, she was about to begin working on the Crumb's kitchen chair. As she laid out the broken pieces on her worktable, she realized that her small toolkit with dowels, glue, and the drill she would need to fix the mortise were not in the store, but at Euphemia's house. She had loaned them to Euphemia a year or so before and hadn't asked for the toolkit to be returned. The rest of her tools were at her old house with Edward. She began to brace herself for her first visit back home when an idea popped into her head. She decided to begin the New Year with a brand-new plan of attack.

Although she'd kept the keys for a year, she'd never put them to use before.

Lou held her breath. It would take her only two minutes to get in and out of Euphemia's.

It was a Thursday night, and she knew Euphemia would be at the town's book club, but she worried that she'd open the front door and find Euphemia with a rolling pin ready to chase 'the burglar' from her house. Lou resisted the urge to count the potted plants on the windowsill and instead moved toward the door as quickly as she could. She rang the doorbell once and then again, and when no one answered, she slid the key into the lock.

Inside, she fought the temptation to run back out the way she'd come in. She reminded herself that this was *not* a break-in; she was simply entering a friend's home to retrieve what was hers. Surely an old friend wouldn't mind if she let herself in to pick up her toolkit. Euphemia need never know.

She sat down on the small wooden bench in the entryway to remove her salt-stained boots, and breathed in the familiar scent of the house. Her mother used to quote Nabokov: *nothing revives the past so completely as the smell that was once associated with it.* The smells of Lou's childhood were pumpkin seeds roasting in the oven, a wooden table warming in the sun, and a strong cup of coffee cooling on the windowsill. Euphemia's house smelled like a combination of Lysol and moist earth. When Lou had first been invited to Euphemia's for tea or sangria, she'd struggled to stomach the smell of the plants. The aroma of growth and fermentation was simply too much.

She'd been inside Euphemia's house many times, but mostly with Edward when they were invited to dinner. They would reheat leftovers for the twins and shuffle across the street to Euphemia's. Every time Euphemia opened the door, she greeted them with a glass of wine in hand and a flour-covered apron that wrapped around her waist twice.

Sitting across the table from Euphemia with Edward to her right, Lou had realized that she wanted to live alone. Euphemia had crow's feet around her eyes, hands hardened from gardening, and a house full of poisonous plants. Lou had never expected to envy that freedom. Lou's children were almost grown and would be leaving for university soon. She didn't want to be left with nothing but her marriage when they went away.

Lou put one hand on the bannister as she rounded the corner and tried to lighten the sound and pressure of her footsteps. She passed the end table with books stacked up the wall: Nicole Brossard (the same edition of *Mauve Desert* that Lou had kept beside her bed and now kept beside her cot), Carol Shields, bell hooks, and Mary Shelley. She reminded herself that she was in the house for a purpose. She glanced at the answering machine—the red light blinked every few seconds. Lou moved towards what Euphemia called her 'amnesia cupboard,' her place for the odds and ends in her home that had nowhere else to go. It was also where she kept her stash of Hobnobs, which she was hardly ever without. Since Euphemia hadn't remembered to return the toolkit, the amnesia cupboard was her best bet.

Lou rounded the corner and halted with her heart in her throat when she saw Euphemia in the armchair, asleep with her mouth open and a half-eaten packet of Hobnobs resting in her lap. As Euphemia breathed, Lou could see each crease and fold in her neck, pleated like an old book.

Lou knew that she needed to get out before Euphemia woke up so no one would ever have to know about her stupid, careless mistake. This could ruin *everything*—her anonymity, any sense of control she was clinging to, her very trustworthiness within Snowton. Lou was prepared to boil this whole incident down to a moment of insanity, but as she turned to leave, she caught her toe on the corner of the wall with the full force of her body weight behind her.

"*Fuck*. Fucking hell," she cried, "fuck, fuck, *fuck*."

She realized her error as soon as the words were out of her mouth, but somehow her exclamation had not roused Euphemia from sleep. Lou should have been discovered as soon as she cried out, which should have been followed by a look of shocked confusion on Euphemia's face. The Hobnobs should have fallen; a hand should have grabbed the rolling pin. But none of this happened.

CHAPTER 7

"Ms. Rosenbaum? Euphemia?"

As Lou crept closer, she confirmed that Euphemia was breathing, but only barely, and there was a gurgling sound like a blocked sink in the space between her inhalations. Lou, wishing that she'd inherited her mother's calm temperament, reached for the phone to dial 9-1-1 but dropped the handset, which sent the batteries rolling across the room and under the couch. She remembered her cell phone in her pocket and pushed the emergency call button from the lock screen.

"9-1-1, what's your emergency?"

"It's my neighbour, I think she's had a heart attack or a stroke or something. She's unconscious."

Lou answered the standard questions while an ambulance was dispatched—she checked for a pulse, counted breaths, held Euphemia's hand, but she wished that the ambulance would materialize and cart Euphemia to the hospital immediately. By the time the paramedics finally arrived, Euphemia's breathing was more laborious, and the gurgles were worsening. Ultimately, it was only seven minutes and twenty-nine seconds between the phone call and the moment when the doorbell rang, but to Lou, it felt like hours had passed.

Lou stayed beside her as the paramedics transferred Euphemia to a stretcher, securing a strap over her chest and across her legs to keep her from rolling off in transit.

"Euphemia?"

Her eyes shifted beneath her lids like mice moving under a carpet.

Lou placed a hand on her friend's foot, the only place she could reach, as they loaded her into the ambulance. Just as the ambulance doors were about to close, Lou saw Euphemia open her eyes halfway and hold Lou's stare for a second or two before closing them again.

"Meet us at the hospital, Ma'am. The doctors will want to ask some questions."

The ambulance pulled out of the crescent with sirens on, leaving Lou shoeless and cold, blood beginning to pool beneath her bruised toenail. The shifting curtains in her old house across the street caught her eye. Edward watched her through the kitchen window with a cup of coffee in his hand and his housecoat wrapped tightly around him. Lou went back inside the house to get her bag and her boots, and to hold the weight of her keys in her hands before driving to the hospital.

CHAPTER 8

Disinfectant, baby powder, and a brief hint of floor cleaner: Lou would have recognized the clinical tang of the hospital blindfolded. She tried breathing in for seven seconds and out for four, an anxiety tip she'd read about online. It had never worked for her, but she needed to do something to calm the thumping in her chest. Her body felt even heavier when she saw that the woman at the information desk was Edward's cousin, Beth. She had brought Lou a cup of tea when she was last at the hospital, but had been frosty with her since Edward told her about the separation. Beth hadn't been there for Thanksgiving, so she got the memo the next day. Lou steeled herself, clenched and unclenched her fists, and continued counting breaths to keep panic from showing on her face.

"Beth, could you tell me where Euphemia Rosenbaum is?"

A brief glance above the top of the computer.

"Oh. It's *you*."

"Euphemia *Rosenbaum*. She should have arrived in an ambulance about ten minutes ago."

Beth blinked slowly as if she didn't understand the question, but Lou knew that although Beth play-acted dullness, it was a ploy to disarm her opponents. She had the skills and ingenuity to be a detective. Lou didn't blame Beth for being protective of her cousin; Lou would probably react the same way in her place.

Beth turned to her computer and began typing.

"Looks like she's in the ICU, but stable. I'll let the doctor know you're here," Beth looked up from her computer fully for the first time and flashed a conspiratorial grin. "What were you doing with that batty old lady, anyway?"

"She's a friend of mine."

"That woman doesn't have friends. Edward told me you only went to her dinners to be polite. What really happened?"

Lou blushed and was trying to formulate an answer when Beth continued, "She didn't try poison you, did she? I heard that's how poor Isabella died. Homemade hemlock tea." The phone rang at her desk.

"She isn't a batty old lady."

Beth asked the caller to hold, placed the handset back in its cradle, and then sighed as she regarded Lou with what looked suspiciously like disdain. "The doctor's on her way. She'll just ask you a few questions about Mrs. Rosenbaum."

"It's Ms. She finds Mrs. diminutive."

"Whatever, Louise."

Lou sat down on one of the chairs with her back to Beth. She needed to project calm. She couldn't show that she was bothered or flustered or that anything was amiss. She rehearsed her story:

The door was open.

I was concerned.

Normally, I wouldn't dream of entering someone's home.

I thought I smelled gas.

The phone rang at the desk as a doctor arrived. Lou stood up, feeling tightness in her back as she gathered her coat and her bag. The doctor was about Lou's age, with her hair pulled into a tight ponytail. Lou didn't recognize her, but she knew that doctors often commuted from Calgary to keep their work and home life separate. Lou was beginning to wish for the same, but she knew she had no one to blame but herself.

"You're Louise Till?"

"I am—I was really concerned about Euphemia." Lou tried to stuff her coat under her arm so she could shake the doctor's hand.

"I won't shake your hand, if that's all right, Ms. Till. It's flu season around here."

Lou pulled her hand back towards her body and felt a trickle of sweat trailing down the small of her back and into the waistband of her jeans. Again, she wished she had her mother's composure, a calm that would allow her to experience stressful situations without excessive perspiration.

"She's stable now. She's lucky you found her when you did," she said.

"What happened?"

"A heart attack. We'll run the standard tests to make sure she's all right, but she's stable for now. She's asleep at the moment, but she was asking for you earlier." The doctor was about to turn when Lou touched her arm.

"Did she say anything?"

"Only that she wanted to see you."

"Her door was wide open—I was concerned."

"Well, it's a good thing you trusted your instincts. Ms. Rosenbaum is lucky you found her when you did."

The doctor turned, and Lou followed her through a maze of corridors and staircases until they reached Euphemia's room. The doctor left, and Lou held onto the doorframe, leaning her body into it. The sight of Euphemia's small body in the hospital bed sent her reeling back to when her mother was the body in the bed, her father in another bed on the other side of the dividing curtain.

A nurse beside Euphemia's bed adjusted IV drip bags. He handled them with a deft touch, one that Lou had certainly never acquired in woodwork, and his movements captivated her. He turned to her, and Lou blushed, embarrassed for staring, but he smiled and gestured to the plastic chair next to the bed.

"Louise, right? She seems to come in and out. If you have time to stay, I'm sure she'd be happy to see you when she wakes up. She's been asking for you."

Lou nodded and draped her jacket across the back of the chair, then sat down, unsure of whether to speak to Euphemia or just let her sleep. When her parents were dying, the doctors and nurses had told her to talk to them, but the doctors knew they wouldn't be waking up, and Lou had thought that speaking to her parents was more for her own sake than for theirs.

Before the nurse left the room, he placed a cup of pudding on the table beside Euphemia. "If you need anything, push this button and a nurse will come."

Alone with Euphemia, Lou leaned forward and exhaled for what felt like the first time in hours. She doubled herself over to put pressure on her chest and continued breathing: in through the nose for seven and out through the mouth for four. Lou brought her body upright as her heart slowed to a normal rate. Her stomach grumbled. Another manifestation of her anxiety was an inexplicable hunger during times of stress. When she was younger and just learning how to drive, she'd return home safe but starving and all but decimate her parents' refrigerator.

She eyed the pudding on the table. Euphemia probably wouldn't be awake for a number of hours—she wouldn't miss her pudding. Lou felt that if she didn't eat something soon, she might faint, and then she'd be no help to anyone. She got hand sanitizer from the dispenser on the wall, lifted the cup and dipped her pointer finger into the pudding, leaving a round indent in the surface.

The moment she brought her finger to her mouth and felt the sugar warming her tongue, she looked up to see Euphemia eyeing her through half shut lids the same way she had in the ambulance. Lou returned the cup of pudding to the table, slowing her movements and controlling her breathing, which had become shallow once again.

"Euphemia, how are you feeling?"

Lou began to wonder if her friend had lost the ability to speak—if the heart attack might have caused a loss of brain function. She watched as Euphemia licked her pruned lips and swallowed, her throat lifting under her spotted skin.

"You broke into my house."

It was a statement. There was no question in her voice.

Lou opened her mouth but no sound came out.

"I don't need to know why. I just need to know if you could do it again."

Lou blinked and tasted the pudding that coated her mouth. She realized she had never swallowed it. "The door was open. I came by to get some flour and when I saw that the door was open, I was concerned, so I knocked, and I pushed it, and then I went in."

"Don't lie to me."

"But—"

"My door was locked."

"But I—"

"The others might believe you, but I don't."

"Euphemia—"

"Could you do it again?"

"But I haven't done anything."

"I am asking you a simple question: could you break into my house again?"

Lou looked down at her salt-stained winter boots and the white woollen socks peeking out from the top; she swallowed the pudding and nodded.

"Well, Louise, I've got a job for you."

And so began the second half of Louise Till's life.

CHAPTER 9

Lou could hardly believe what Euphemia was asking when she made her proposition in the hospital. At first, Lou wondered if Euphemia's rational thinking skills had been affected by the heart attack. But she was in full control of her faculties as always, despite it being just a few short hours since she had been found comatose. Lou struggled to keep up with what Euphemia was saying, but she soon understood what was being asked of her.

"I'm the only one who knows Isabella was murdered," Euphemia said in a low conspiratorial tone.

"But the doctors said it was old age."

"Doctors aren't saints, you know. They lie."

"And how do you know for sure?"

"Trust me, I know."

"But surely—"

"I know what I'm talking about."

"I'm not saying you're wrong, it's just a big leap to think Isabella was murdered when the doctors say she died of natural causes."

"Did you know that her necklace was missing?"

Lou shook her head.

"Isabella *never* took that necklace off. Not to sleep. Not to shower. Never. Someone must have poisoned her or smothered her with a pillow, then ripped it from her neck."

"So, you think whoever killed her has the necklace."

"Precisely."

"But what do you want me to do?"

"Now you're asking the right questions. I've been narrowing down a list of suspects for the past eight months. You're going to break into their houses the way you broke into mine and find the necklace."

"But, Euphemia, I'd never broken into anyone's house before today," Lou paused to catch her breath. "I'm not a criminal."

"Well, you are now. Don't make me threaten you, Louise. Don't make me tell everyone that you've been planning this for years."

"But I haven't been planning anything." Lou's heart was beginning to beat like the vibrating motors she stocked in the store.

"Yes, but they don't know that, do they?" A patient from down the hall began coughing and crying out for a nurse. "You may go now. I'll be in touch."

Incredulous, Lou lifted herself from the chair. She felt like she was floating. Within seconds Euphemia began to snore. The sound trailed down the hallway as Lou made for the hospital lobby. Her clothes hung on her body and felt heavier than before.

What could she do? She could refuse to have anything to do with Euphemia's plan, and her secret would be exposed to her children, to her friends, to everyone. She'd be a social pariah.

Or she could go along with it, dig into Euphemia's suspicions. Lou had always known it was just a matter of time before her key cutting got her into trouble. Her head was still spinning when she reached the lobby, and her heart sank even further because Edward was sitting there, looking utterly out of place. He got to his feet when Lou rounded the corner and stepped in front of her to keep her from walking by without acknowledging him.

"What happened? Is she all right?"

Lou shot Beth a look to say, *How could you?* but Beth barely looked up from her computer monitor.

"A minor heart attack. She's stable, but it looks like she'll be in the hospital for a bit."

"I can't believe it." Lou wondered if the shock on Edward's face was genuine, or if this was an audition for him. He was trying to show the great depths of emotion he was capable of; but it was too little, and he was too late.

"She'll be fine. I'll come and visit her every day."

"I'll join you, if that's all right."

"I'd prefer if you didn't."

There was a moment when neither of them said anything. Lou was about to leave when Edward continued.

"Beth said she was pretty looped when they first brought her in. She was talking about keys and door locks like there was a conspiracy against her or something. We thought she might finally be off her rocker."

Lou could see that Edward was trying not to chuckle. So much for the audition.

"What do you want, Edward?"

He deflated a little. "I want to help. I thought that after your parents . . . that being back here might be hard for you."

"So, you want to be supportive?"

"I do."

"Then stay out of my way and let me take care of her."

Lou readjusted the strap of her bag and pushed past him to the revolving doors. She didn't want or need his support. She would handle Euphemia on her own.

CHAPTER 10

Two weeks later, a letter written in pen across three hospital napkins arrived at the hardware store.

SUSPECTS

(The order and contents of this list may be amended if new information comes to light):

- Bart Hastings (The man writes murder mysteries for a living, and let me tell you, he's been running out of ideas. You know what he told me his next book was going to be called? *Murder Most Fowl.* Someone found dead in a chicken coop. I wouldn't put it past him to commit a real murder so he could get a plot for his next book.)

- Phillip Dion (I've known Phillip a long time, much longer than you have. The man has debts: gambling debts, overdrawn bank accounts, and overdue library books—I know about all of them. You've seen him around town with his metal detector, poking under rocks in the park checking for spare change. The man is like a magpie. If it shines, he's already got his hands in your pockets.)

- Ben and Indigo Higgins (I think she's hiding something under those long, flowing skirts of hers. Besides, who needs that many garden gnomes if they aren't hiding something? Mercury is no longer in retrograde—who knows what she's capable of?)

- Frank Blake (He has been the most insistent that Isabella died from natural causes. He thinks he's a crime scene investigator from how much he talks about autopsies, ballistics, DNA profiling, and Luminal. I don't think he knows what any of it means.)

- Mark and Beth Dull (As a family member, I think she might be an accomplice for your ~~husband~~ ex-husband.)

- Edward Till (This will be the most interesting. Why do you think I invited you to all of those damn dinners?)

PROCEDURE:

1. Ring the doorbell of each suspect. If someone answers, pull a coupon out of your pocket and explain that there is a paint promotion for the store and then leave. Offer coupons to all surrounding neighbours in order to avoid suspicion.

2. If no one answers, do a preliminary check of the area. If all is clear, let yourself in (you know how to do this).

3. Once you are inside, close and lock the door behind you and keep your ears open for someone coming in. If there are children in the home, leave and come back later. We don't need to traumatize anyone (even ankle biters).

4. Check anywhere you think valuables may be hidden. Remember, you are looking for the necklace. We find the necklace, we find our killer.

5. Do not get distracted.

6. Do not perform any home repairs while you are in someone else's house.

7. Leave the way you came and do not leave a trace of your visit.

8. Remember, you are doing a kindness for an old woman with the ability and means to blackmail you. There should be no guilt involved.

9. Remember, not a word to anyone.

Your new partner in crime,
   Euphemia

Fall

CHAPTER 11

It was back in October when Lou got a splinter in her finger
from a piece of plywood. The finger became infected before
long—the splinter ached beneath the skin, which began to
ooze after many removal attempts. Lou didn't want to be
melodramatic, but she considered the splinter the beginning of
the end of her old life. Before the snow fell, before the break-in,
before the blackmail, before she lived out of her hardware store,
Lou tapped her aching finger against the steering wheel as she
delivered fifteen grade A and five utility-grade turkeys to the
community hall and noticed that the leaves had turned from
yellow to deep amber. Most of the leaves had fallen from their
branches and had become mulch beneath the tires of her car.

She knew she should have delivered the turkeys days before,
but she'd been working on a project for the hardware store and
preparations for the dinner had entirely slipped her mind. As
she was putting the finishing brushes on a knife block stained
to a walnut shade, she remembered her promise to deliver
twenty turkeys to the community hall by three o'clock that
afternoon.

Lou drove from Snowton to Calgary and then to what
seemed like every grocery store in Calgary. She found most
of the stores were sold out of turkeys. She did manage to pick
up one or two turkeys at some stores. She finally conceded
she would need to buy a few utility turkeys, and she asked to
see whatever turkeys they had left. The store managers pulled
turkeys that hadn't been suitable for the main freezer cases out
of back storeroom freezers; Lou gratefully took whatever they

had. Once they were transferred from the cart to the car, the turkeys rolled around in the hatch and knocked against one another like high heels on an icy sidewalk. The sound reminded her of a story her father used to tell every Thanksgiving.

Her father was born and raised in Snowton, but commuted to downtown Calgary for a time while Lou was growing up. She and her mother had run the hardware store. The economy meant that fewer people were doing home repairs or commissioning woodwork for their homes. There was hardly enough work in town for a handyman, so Lou's father topped up his income with office work in Calgary to keep the store afloat and the family fed. He received a holiday bonus each year until the economic downturn really hit, and the oil company could no longer afford bonuses. Not wanting to send their employees away completely empty-handed for the holidays, they decided to give Christmas turkeys as a token of good will. Each worker received a twenty-pound frozen turkey—with cooking instructions—to take home. Her father described the scenes in the streets: men in suits trying to haul frozen turkeys, loading them into cabs the way they would a small child, turkeys slipping from their grip and gliding across the snowy pavement. Some left their turkeys on the sidewalks, unwilling to commute with the beasts under their arms. Lou imagined that if her father were in the passenger seat, he wouldn't be able to help himself, and he would tell the story again, and she would laugh, again.

Lou had spent the last months on commissioned pieces that her parents had committed to. She couldn't predict how she would feel when she completed the list of her parents' projects. She didn't know if anyone would commission new pieces from her. She'd never had the soft and controlled touch that her parents had with woodworking. She'd never had a soft and controlled touch with anything, for that matter.

When Lou entered the community hall through the gymnasium doors, the first smell that she recognized was burnt stuffing; the acrid scent of blackened bread hung in the air. The aroma reminded Lou of her mother and how she always looked too large for her kitchen with her brightly coloured apron and her hair sticking out and curling up from the heat of the oven. This was Lou's first year coordinating the dinner and her first Thanksgiving without her parents.

She was rattled by how keenly she felt her grief. She hadn't expected to experience more grief at Thanksgiving than on any other day—she'd anticipated that as an adult with children of her own she would be prepared for her parents to die, but their sudden and mysterious deaths had caught her completely off guard. She batted off comments about weight loss and how good she looked. She didn't want to lose weight; she'd lost it because all of her body's energies and nutrients were supporting her grief. She tried to push away thoughts of her parents and to focus on the coming task: on top of swallowing her grief like mouthfuls of candied yam, she had a decision to make. She'd kept herself busy preparing for the dinner and keeping the store afloat, but it was nearing time to decide.

Eve barrelled through the swinging kitchen doors with her glasses fogged and a ladle pointed in Lou's direction.

"Did you get enough turkeys?"

It was 2:54 in the afternoon. She could breathe easy and release the tension in her shoulders, knowing that she'd more or less come through.

"I got twenty."

"And you got whole cranberry sauce, right? Not jellied?"

"Yes, just like you asked for," Lou said. As the kitchen doors swung back and forth, she saw Al, Eve's son, with his index finger digging into a metal bowl full of frosting. He'd obviously been waiting for his mother to leave the kitchen to sneak a taste. Lou had enlisted as much help as she possibly could: Eve, Wanda, and Bart were managing the kitchen. She'd also volunteered her children to keep them busy and out of the house over their fall holiday. Thanksgiving dinner often saw two hundred people coming through the doors. As the kitchen doors swung, she saw her son join Al and slide his finger into the bowl of icing. Lou had wondered if and when Al and Stewart might become a couple. She'd seen the way they were together, and she was hopeful that her son might avoid heartache in his teenage years by falling in love with his best friend. She hoped that Eve felt the same, but she could never get a clear reading of Eve's impression of the boys.

Eve's tortoiseshell glasses slid down her nose as she shook her head. "It's our first year without your mother, and I refuse to be made a fool of by a turkey dinner."

She and Eve had grown up together, and as long as Lou had known her, Eve had kept her glasses on a chain around her neck like a librarian, fiddling with them when she was nervous and tapping an arm against her cheek when she was trying to think. Lou resisted reminding her about the year that Frank Blake ruined the dinner. He had been describing the 'Mr. Bean Christmas skit,' and demonstrated it by placing the turkey on his head. As could be expected, the pelvic bones of the turkey were just wide enough to reach around his head, but once it was on, he couldn't pull it off. He'd come lumbering out of the kitchen like Frankenstein, stinking of stuffing and innards. Lou's mother had refused to let him anywhere near the kitchen the next year.

Lou anticipated that Eve might not find the story entertaining under the circumstances, and so she kept it to herself. "Eve, what could possibly go wrong?"

"You'd better knock on wood, my dear."

Lou reached across her to the wood paneling on the wall and tapped three times. "Happy now?"

"Ecstatic."

Eve smiled, and her eyes crinkled; her glasses had cleared, and she placed a hand on Lou's shoulder. Eve could be harsh at times (she just had to look at Al to see the tight leash she'd kept him on all these years), but she also knew that Eve had loved Lou's mother as much as anyone else in town.

It was *everyone's* first Thanksgiving without her.

Eve squeezed Lou's arm one last time and returned to the kitchen where she would find the boys and confiscate the bowl of frosting.

Lou went out to her SUV to bring in the last of the turkeys. She hoped to hide the 'lesser turkeys' beneath the A Grades, but she knew they'd be seen eventually. As she carted the last of the turkeys through the doors and went back to shut the hatch, a familiar car pulled into the parking lot, her husband behind the steering wheel.

"Did you get enough turkeys?" Edward was rolling down the window as he spoke, so Lou only caught the last half of his question. She bit the inside of her cheek, put on her brightest smile and said, "Yes."

"Great. I told you there was nothing to worry about," he said.

She bit the inside of her cheek, again, harder this time, until she felt her eyes begin to water from the sharp pain.

Edward unbuckled his seatbelt, opened his car door and reached to put his arms around her. He obviously thought she was going to cry. As he held her, he smoothed down the hair on the back of her head with his winter gloves and held her face against his Gore-Tex covered chest. She knew there was a time when she had found this comforting, but now she felt her cheeks beginning to flame from the warmth, and she felt a pinch in her shoulder as he squeezed it.

"I know this has been a hard week for you. It's been hard on all of us."

Lou nodded and looked over her husband's shoulder to count the number of bricks in the side of the community hall. By the time he loosened his arms, she'd counted thirty-seven.

"Just remember that we're all with you."

She nodded into his chest and felt the material of his jacket scraping her cheeks as she began to pull away from his embrace.

"I should really get the last of these turkeys inside."

The skin under Edward's eyes was darker than usual. He hadn't been sleeping, but then, neither had she. Most nights, she felt his weight shift from the bed as he got up, took his fleece housecoat off the hook from behind the door, and moved into the living room to read. He never woke the kids, and she was grateful for that.

"Louise?"

She lifted a hand to her face to keep the wind from blowing her hair into her eyes.

"What?"

"I love you."

She nodded, smiled, and wrapped her scarf a little tighter around her throat.

"Tomorrow will be fine. I know it will," she said to herself like a mantra as she carted the last of the turkeys inside.

*****

The night of the dinner, Lou took in everything happening around her. Edward lit tea candles for each table. Stewart and Molly wrapped orange and brown streamers around concrete pillars. Eve straightened the corners of tablecloths. Under his mother's direction, Al used a metre stick to check that the place settings were straight. Bart talked to himself, probably mapping the plot of his next thriller. Some of the neighbourhood children sat gathered in a corner, tracing their hands with scented markers on orange construction paper to make turkeys. She heard Molly talking with her father across the room and couldn't avoid listening in on the conversation.

"I don't know why we celebrate Thanksgiving. It's just a holdover from colonialism in America," she said.

Edward paused his candle lighting because the lighter began to flicker. He shook it a little too vigorously and accidentally hit the table. "Yes," he said slowly, "but at least there's turkey."

Edward, uncomfortable and fully out of his depth, handed Molly a set of streamers and asked her to decorate the other side of the gym. Lou agreed with her daughter, and voiced the same opinion to Edward each year. She suspected that at least part of his discomfort arose from how much Molly sounded like her mother.

Lou left her watching place to look at the photos on the walls. Each Thanksgiving dinner since the town had come into existence was pictured with the same characters and supporting cast over entire lifetimes as they crossed and intersected with one another. She didn't need to search for her parents' faces. She knew their exact placement in each photo: her mother was at the back left with Lou's father next to her. Most years, they were in the same pose. Her mother had been taller than Lou's father by a foot, and she stood with her elbow resting on his shoulder as he smiled his snaggletooth grin and looked at her instead of at the camera. Lou's favourite photo was the first one they appeared in together. Her mother had slipped her hand into his just as the shutter clicked, immortalizing with her wide-set smile and his look of awe their first moments as a couple. They were in their early twenties, and they were in love.

Lou was pulled out of her daydreaming by Eve's voice and a metal bowl of stuffing clattering to the floor. This town was her home. It had always been her home. These people were her family and had been her parents' family; and yet, she couldn't keep her mind on Thanksgiving preparations, and she did not have the energy to be enthusiastic about another holiday. Everything would be the same as it always was. Her husband would try too hard to be entertaining and would inevitably tell the same stories as the year before. Someone, probably Phillip, would bring a flask to spike the punch, and the adults (plus a few teenagers) would end up drinking more than they could handle. They would be smuggled from the gymnasium, citing an upset stomach. Someone would inevitably say, "I hope it wasn't the turkey."

They all grew older, but nothing ever changed. She buttoned her coat, planning to slip outside and go for a walk, when she felt someone sidle up beside her.

"Multa salvete. Si vestri, bene ergo quod est bene et optime ego quoque."

"What language are you learning now, Euphemia?"

"Latin. That means: Many greetings. If you're well, then that's good, and I'm well too."

"What happened to learning Hungarian?"

"I've already learned it," Euphemia unwrapped her scarf from her neck and unbuttoned her pea coat. "And are you well?"

"I'm as well as I can be."

Euphemia seemed satisfied with this answer as she handed Lou her scarf and coat. In her arms, she carried a bag of plant leaves that Lou didn't recognize.

"You look upset."

"I'm fine, Euphemia. Really."

Lou moistened her lips, which had suddenly turned dry as wood chips.

"The first one is always the hardest. Trust me."

Lou initially assumed that she referred solely to her parents but then she remembered that this was Euphemia's first Thanksgiving without Isabella.

"I suppose it's not *just* my parents I'm thinking about . . ."

Before Euphemia could answer, another bowl of stuffing clattered to the floor across the hall, followed by a holler from Eve.

"You have something in your teeth, my dear." Lou felt around with her tongue but had no idea what might be in between her teeth or where she should even look. "Grief is no excuse for poor dental hygiene, Louise."

Lou made a mental note of that. It sounded profound, even if it wasn't much help to her.

"Omnibus bene tibi erit."

"What does that mean?"

"All will be well," Euphemia said.

She watched as Euphemia shuffled across the hall toward the kitchen, her bag of leaves held firmly in her hands.

*****

The dinner had gone as smoothly as she could have hoped. Eve hadn't mentioned anything about the turkeys that were missing wings or had strange pockmarks along their backs. Indigo Higgins had gotten up to the microphone to sing the *Charlie Brown Thanksgiving* song a capella, and before she left the stage, she said that Mercury was no longer in retrograde, so they should take this time to be happy with friends and family while they could. Lou kept an eye on Phillip, who had stashed his metal detector under the table, and, as she'd predicted, pulled a flask from his coat pocket to fortify his cup of punch. Though they were almost grown up, her kids still sat at the children's table, probably out of habit more than any self-identification.

The conversations and interactions were like clockwork. She'd known these people all her life, their quirks and oddities never cause for concern, but she'd begun to feel like her track saw—completely stuck in place. The dinner, thankfully, was almost over, and Lou was examining the tray of desserts at the centre of the table. In reality, she wasn't thinking about desserts at all, but, rather, found it easier to stare at the tray of cookies than to risk looking up at her husband.

"Lou?"

She ran her tongue across the back of her teeth and willed herself not to look in his direction. This was not the time.

"Louise?" She knew she had to look up at him. "Your eyes could burn a hole in that dessert tray."

"I'm trying to decide . . ."

Across the table, Phillip Dion was telling his joke about Mussolini that no one listened to anymore.

"You know you don't have to choose between desserts. You're allowed to have more than one."

"That's not what I mean. I—"

Euphemia's eyes widened as she lifted a crooked finger in Edward's direction.

"It's a murder, you know."

"What?" Edward asked. Lou couldn't decide if she heard panic or annoyance in his voice.

"When there's that many of them, you call it a murder."

She was pointing to the window just behind Edward's shoulder. Twelve crows perched on the fence in the lamplight outside the community hall, probably drawn by the scent of stuffing and turkey.

Edward unclenched his jaw and caught his breath while Euphemia smiled slyly. At the other end of the table, Phillip pounded a fist on the tabletop for emphasis in a moment of passionate joke telling, catching the tray with his knuckles and sending the silver tray and remaining turkey pieces clattering to the floor. From where she sat, Lou could see grease marks on the gymnasium floor, along with gravy, stuffing, and turkey bones. One of the turkey frills (that Lou had always thought were strangely gratuitous) continued to roll until it was directly beside her husband's shoe.

"You *fool*," Eve spoke so softly that it was clear to everyone how angry she was.

"I didn't mean to!"

Eve made a sound that made it obvious she wanted to say something far worse, but held her tongue to keep from swearing in polite company.

"Besides," said Phillip, "everyone was finished eating!"

"That does not mean I want to see my turkey flying across the room."

Silence enveloped the table for a few moments, and Lou was grateful for distraction and the reprieve from conversation with her husband.

Euphemia broke the silence, "You know, in 1876, it rained meat for a few hours in Kentucky. They called it the 'Great Kentucky Meat Shower.' At first, everyone thought the meat was human flesh. In fairness, it *was* 1876. It's most likely that a flock of vultures had feasted more abundantly than wisely, and were passing overhead, when they vomited. A few farmers tried the meat and decided it was mutton."

She reached for the tray of desserts and picked a bird's nest cookie from the top. "It's true, look it up if you don't believe me."

Edward, ever the pragmatist, said, "But how could that many vultures regurgitate at the same time? That can't be right."

"It's what all the newspapers said."

"I'll bet the whole thing was meant to scare people off their property, like a hoax."

"I can show you the articles, Edward, if you don't believe me," she looked down at the leftover bits of turkey and bone on the floor, "but they say they tested the meat and found lung and cardiovascular tissues that were similar to human organs. That's why they thought it was people."

A collective shudder rounded the table, and Maya, who chewed like a chipmunk and had been finishing off her last piece of turkey, slowly returned her fork to her plate.

His momentary embarrassment over, Phillip decided to join in. "I heard from a friend of a friend that a pack of vultures still passes over on its migration path—right about this time of year too. You might want to lock up your cattle and bring your pies in off the windowsill."

"Vultures actually have gut bacteria that's toxic to all other animals. It's what keeps them from getting sick when they eat carrion," Edward said.

"Please, I cannot tolerate talk of vultures and carrion at the dinner table," said Eve.

"They've evolved to the point that they can't get sick. So how could a whole pack of vultures vomit simultaneously?"

Lou cleared her throat, wishing that she could ask her husband not to challenge Euphemia so much, but knowing that she wouldn't. While she agreed that Euphemia was a bit of a handful, there was no reason to fight with her at the Thanksgiving dinner, especially about something as trivial as vomiting vultures. Besides, Euphemia was still smiling after getting a rise out of Edward. She enjoyed this. Lou lifted her purse from where it rested between her feet and reached into a side pocket for her keys, to twist them on her carabineer until her sweating hands had touched the key of each person at the table.

#22. Frank Blake
#47. Euphemia Rosenbaum
#49. Our key
#56. Wanda and Lesley Alpin
#102. Bart Hastings
#111. Eve Crumb
#137. Phillip Dion
#189. Maya Holmes

"Edward, can we talk in private?"

He didn't seem to hear her. He was still talking about the vultures.

"*Edward.*" She continued to count.

She'd hoped to distract herself from what she had to do next, but when she reached Maya's key, the words were out of her mouth before she could swallow them back.

"I want a divorce."

She felt all heads at the table turn in her direction, and she found herself experiencing a separation between her brain and her body. She reached for a cookie, suddenly ravenous.

At first it seemed as though Edward hadn't heard her; he smiled the same wide grin that used to remind her of her father's but now looked nothing like him. She watched his reaction in slow motion. He blinked lazily, and with each blink his smile dropped further until his lips formed a straight line.

"You want a divorce?"

"I do."

Eve turned to the others, "We should give them some privacy."

To which Euphemia responded, "We will do no such thing."

"You want a divorce?" Edward asked again. His smile was now completely gone. He stood up from the table, scraping the feet of his metal chair against the gymnasium floor. The rogue turkey frill rolled. "We're not discussing this here."

"I'm not going home."

Edward picked up his napkin to clear up his crumbs, dropped the napkin onto his plate, and left the gymnasium.

From across the table, Lou heard Wanda Alpin turn to Frank and say, "I'd like to divorce my husband too, but I certainly wouldn't do it *here*."

*****

Lou stayed until the twins were ready to leave. As she drove them home, they sat in stunned silence. Even from the children's table, they'd heard what happened. She didn't need to explain. Lou drove them home and went inside the house only long enough to pack some clothes, a bag full of books, Magician, and the cat's necessary supplies. She left the house without a doubt in her mind that she'd done what she needed to do. There was no yelling, only resignation at the fact that the wheels had begun to turn.

Second Winter

CHAPTER 12

Lou took a week to reach a decision—a few days later she went to Bart Hastings' house. She was five minutes away when her focus began to swim, and she had to pull over into a nearby parking lot.

She remembered parking in the same lot once before, after an argument with Edward. The twins were eight then, both crying over a hamster that Lou had stepped on days before, and it was the hottest night of the summer. Thankfully, Lou had been wearing slippers when she stepped on the hamster; she didn't need to pluck small bones from the arch of her foot. She remembered leaving the house in her nightgown and slippers and driving until she reached the lot. She hadn't grabbed her housecoat before driving away, and the sweat on her skin was cold and clammy despite the temperature being in the high thirties. She got into the car alone, but Edward followed her into the garage and closed the garage door from the remote on the wall. She pushed the button again from inside the car, and the door rose, but Edward hadn't closed the door to the house behind him, and Magician seized the opportunity to make a run for it. Lou rolled down the window to raise the alarm about the cat when Edward slid into the back seat and fastened his seatbelt.

"Nothing has to change, Louise. I made a mistake, a big one, but I love you. I love our children. I love our life together."

The cat hopped up onto the hood of the car and began rubbing against the windshield. Lou could hear purring through the open window.

"Get the cat off my car, Edward."

"The cat can wait."

"I'll drive over it."

(They both knew she wouldn't.)

"For fuck's sake, Edward—"

She pressed the car horn and leaned on it while Edward stared at her from the back seat.

"Louise, you're going to wake the neighbours."

She leaned on the horn for a few more seconds, and then slowly let her hand return to her lap. In the rearview mirror, she saw lights flicker on down the street, and she saw Euphemia pressed against the screen door with a bag of Hobnobs in her hand as she watched what she surely knew was an unfolding argument.

"Edward," she said more calmly than she knew she could, "get out of my car, get the cat back inside, and both of you stay there."

She looked straight ahead and placed her hands on the steering wheel as her knuckles turned white.

"She doesn't mean *anything* to me," he said with a heavy exhalation.

The next movements happened quite slowly, as if they were being filmed and slowed down in a studio. He moved his hands to unbuckle his seatbelt and stepped out of the car, lifted the cat off the hood, and then stood in the doorway of their house. Lou watched him holding the cat under his arm like a football, as his glasses slid down his face from the heat. She put the car in reverse and drove until she reached the parking lot.

She had to recalibrate. Her only regret was that she'd threatened to run over Magician and then left her with Edward. The cat deserved better. Lou leaned back in the seat and stared at the wooden fence ahead of her and at the trees in the field beyond. She looked for patterns in the formation of bark and managed to see the faint outline of a pair of eyes and a mouth. She looked down at the steering wheel, and when she glanced at the tree once again, she'd lost her focus and couldn't find the mouth and eyes that had seemed so solid only moments before.

Now, years after the argument, and in the same parking lot, she recalibrated again. Lou put on her sunglasses, turned up the radio, put the car in drive, and reviewed her plan for how she would break into Bart's house.

CHAPTER 13

Euphemia had told her that Bart usually went out for a run with the 'chums' most evenings between five and seven.

Lou had seen him running around town at night, but she was still convinced that if she knocked on his door, she would find him at home in his housecoat. Lou wasn't sure whether she'd rather find Bart in or out. If he opened the door, she wouldn't have to go through with this ridiculous plan of Euphemia's. She parked two blocks away from his house so that no one would spot a strange car in his driveway. Besides, if he did answer the door, her plan to deliver coupons would be far more plausible on foot. As she left the car, her steering wheel glistened with sweat from her hands. She counted her steps the whole way from her car to the front door. Each time she wiped her palms against her pants, they seemed to sweat more and more.

Lou knew exactly which key she needed for Bart's house, and she'd reread Euphemia's instructions multiple times to avoid making careless mistakes. She was as ready as she would ever be, but was still trying to understand how she'd gotten herself into this situation in the first place. A year ago, she'd been a daughter, a wife, a mother, but now she didn't belong anywhere. She'd not only extricated herself from her previous life, but at present she was living someone else's—the life of someone impulsive and someone very unlike her old self. If her parents could see her now.

She rang the doorbell and waited a minute for Bart to answer, listening for sounds of movement from inside. When no such sounds came, she put on her glove and slid her key into the lock as neatly as if it were her own. She found that she was no longer sweating, her heart rate had slowed, and she felt fully in control of her body and her movements. She twisted the doorknob, and, with one final glance behind her, pushed the door open with her shoulder. As she searched for a light switch with her gloved hand, she accidentally flipped on the porch light, but quickly rectified her mistake and closed the door behind her. The mat directly inside the door seemed brand new, and Lou wondered if Bart had ever set foot on it with dirty shoes, or if he took his shoes off before entering the house.

The blinds were open, and light streamed through the windows. The setting sun still came through the window screens; there was wood panelling everywhere and an overwhelming smell of cedar, so strong she was surprised she'd never detected the scent on Bart when she saw him. A white long-haired cat lounged on a yellow pillow propped into the corner of the couch. It seemed unwilling to move its corpulent body even for an intruder.

Lou began her search with the most obvious place: the jewellery box on the coffee table. She lifted the lid, and a tiny mermaid spun in a slow circle in time to "Under the Sea." She dug through costume jewelry and opened all the small drawers, but did not see a necklace matching Euphemia's description. Since Bart was unmarried and never had children, the music box was an odd possession. Lou realized how little she knew about Bart. *Had* he ever been married? Did he have grandchildren who lived elsewhere? Lou had bought his novels, but she had never actually read one. Instantly, she felt worse than she had anticipated for breaking into his house. From the bookshelf on the opposite wall, she took one copy of his latest novel and tucked it into her purse. Surely, he wouldn't mind if a friend borrowed a copy. She looked again at the bookshelves to find that there was no Austen, no Brontë, no Tolstoy—only Bart Hastings. With a tut of her tongue, she spaced the other books on the shelf to make it appear that none were missing; she doubted that he would notice the theft with so many identical copies of *The Typewriter Murders*. Out of curiosity, she counted them—one hundred and four copies of his own novel. A vanity wall. His novels were placed on the shelf in chronological order, at least a few hundred in total—all his own books.

She checked less obvious places next: the kitchen cookie jar, the freezer (she knew that people often wrapped valuables in tin foil), the cupboards, where she found hundreds of cans of Fancy Feast, beneath the potted plant on the coffee table, the linen closet. When Lou felt that she had exhausted all of the options she was willing to explore—she refused to search his bathroom garbage—she picked up her coat from the couch and began to leave the way she came in. As she turned back around to face the door, the long-haired cat leapt from the couch and entangled itself between her legs. To avoid crushing the cat's paws, she reached out an arm to lean against a wall, but instead, knocked over the vase filled with daisies that sat on the table.

The vase must have been weak to begin with, since it shattered when it struck the floor. Thankfully, the moisture that soaked into the rug was clear, but there was no way Lou could get it dry and cleaned up before Bart returned from his run. Lou assessed her options. It was unlikely that he had a hair dryer, and she couldn't leave dirty towels and broken glass that hadn't been there when he left in his hamper. She decided to wet her hands in the remaining water and rub what moisture she could onto the cat's fur so that it might seem as though the cat had knocked over the vase and rolled around in the water afterwards. The cat hissed at her, upset at being both disturbed and wet. Once the cat was sufficiently wet, it wandered back to its cushion on the couch, licked itself, and fell asleep.

Lou knew that she'd made a mistake that could ruin her chances at keeping her secret. And, she had done all of this for nothing.

Before leaving, she put her eye to the peephole to make sure no one was coming up the drive, and then let herself out the same way she'd come in. She locked the door behind her and expected to be sweaty, panicked, at least uncomfortable with the crime she'd just committed. But no. Lou was tranquil in a way she hadn't felt since her father had held her hands against the thumb turns on his old key cutter, almost as if the same vibrations juddered through her bones.

CHAPTER 14

The day after searching Bart's house, Lou went to the hospital. When she entered the room, Euphemia dropped her hand to her side and looked to the doorway with wide eyes. Her face relaxed when she saw who it was.

"Oh, it's just you. Be a dear and open the window?"

Lou had spent enough hours in stuffy hospital rooms to know that there was no way to coax the windows open.

"I don't think they can open."

"No matter."

Euphemia reached behind her pillow and pulled out an electronic cigarette. With long, bony fingers, she slipped it between her lips. The action was so seamless, it was clear she had rehearsed and practised often. Her hands were as steady as Lou's had been at the Hastings' house. Lou could do nothing but stand and stare, amazed by Euphemia's gall, vaping in a hospital room. In response, Euphemia looked at her with one eyebrow raised.

"Well? Did you find the necklace?"

"No."

"*Damn.*"

Lou sat down in the chair and hesitated before saying, "And I broke a vase."

"Louise. Do you *want* to get caught?" The disappointment on Euphemia's face was obvious.

"No, but—"

"You cannot be so careless. I'd go myself if I could get out of this damn hospital room, but they've got me under lock and key. Pardon the pun."

"He's not your killer, anyway. No necklace. He just keeps cat food like the apocalypse is coming and has hundreds of his own books on his shelves. Did you know that he has a vanity wall? I suppose I don't know any other authors, but a vanity wall just seems so . . . vain."

"Are you really surprised by that?" She took another drag. "I guess Bart must not be as desperate for a new idea as I'd guessed."

A thought popped into Lou's head that had nothing to do with the investigation, but intrigued her nonetheless.

"I think he's been ordering his own books. He made the provincial bestseller list last year, and no one in town even knew what his book was about. Maybe he's been buying them all himself."

Euphemia nodded, obviously pleased to have *some* information, but it wasn't the information she really wanted.

"I just wish the damned doctors would let me have some of my plants in here. My poor foxglove must be dying at home."

"They probably think you'll try to kill yourself if they let you bring in poisonous plants. Or that you'll try to kill them."

"Humph, what do they know? If I wanted to kill the doctors or nurses, I could do it with something in this room. These handy wires all around the bed wouldn't be too bad for garroting."

Lou wasn't sure how to respond to Euphemia's grisly cheer.

"Of course, you're right. A little light murder would be easier if I had my plants here. Just a sprinkle of nightshade or hemlock, and *presto,* dead as a doornail."

Not for the first time, Lou wondered if she were being led on a mission by a woman who was out of her mind. She decided to return to the initial conversation and try to extricate herself entirely. She would leave the hospital and make a clean break.

"I could water your plants for you if you like—but I can't break into any more houses. It feels wrong letting myself into someone else's house."

"You didn't seem to have any issues letting yourself into mine."

"That was different. You wouldn't be alive if I hadn't."

"Am I supposed to thank you for that?"

"You might consider it."

"Louise, may I remind you of the precariousness of your situation in this town? Your recent separation from your dolt of a husband, while I *personally* support it wholeheartedly, has made you the subject of some unkind gossip."

"I can handle that."

"You haven't done a very good job of handling it so far."

"Besides, people get divorced all the time. It shouldn't be newsworthy."

"Oh, Louise. If that's really what you think, you don't know the people of Snowton at all." Lou didn't say anything in response, because she was learning that she *didn't* really know the people who lived in Snowton. "Besides," Euphemia continued, "no one can blame an old lady if she accidentally lets some sensitive information slip to her fellow townsfolk, can they?"

Lou took a deep breath. She could give her one more house, but that was it.

"Fine. Who's next on the list?"

Euphemia smiled at Lou, who was sitting cross-legged on the chair, but it wasn't an unkind smile. If anything, it was the smile of a jokester for whom every moment is one great performance.

Lou began to wonder if Euphemia hadn't been planning something like this for quite some time. She had been trapped by a superior intelligence.

Euphemia lifted herself with her elbows to readjust her position in the hospital bed. "You know who's next. And be careful when you're watering my foxglove, dear. You'll want to wear a mask so you don't inhale any spores."

That evening, when Lou went to Euphemia's to water and prune the plants, she was surprised to find the damp, earthy scent of the house almost comforting. She took the opportunity to look around; she was alone in Euphemia's house, and there were no foreseeable medical emergencies this time. If Euphemia was going to blackmail her, Lou should start looking for some kind of ammunition. She didn't know what form that ammunition might take, but there had to be something untoward in Euphemia's house.

The house looked exactly the same as the first time Lou had let herself in; the stack of books hadn't changed, the plants were wilting only slightly, and the light on the answering machine continued to flash. Lou hit play, and Euphemia's voice came through. After the beep, Lou heard something she hadn't expected.

"Hi Phemy, it's me. Give me a ring when you have a second, there's something I want to talk to you about."

It took Lou a moment to place why she knew the voice and then she realized: Isabella. A robotic voice on the answering machine said, *Message received three hundred and seven days ago. Message will be deleted in four days. Press nine to save message for twenty-one more days.* Lou pressed nine, watered the plants, and went back to her hardware store.

CHAPTER 15

Lou waited another two weeks before attempting the second break-in. She didn't want to go through with it. How could she resist being blackmailed? And what could Euphemia really do, after all?

But the pressure was relentless. Five mornings straight, small brown envelopes had been stuffed under the hardware store's door. Inside were more hospital napkins with illustrations of keys and various forms of *you know what you have to do, Louise.* Lou wondered who Euphemia enlisted to deliver the notes. Enclosed in the final envelope was a letter from Euphemia explaining that she had been released from the hospital on the condition that she not smoke or drink, and that she return to the hospital once a week for a check-up. Even though these conditions were agreed to, Lou knew that Euphemia wouldn't be within a mile of the hospital if she could avoid it. Since she'd received news of her discharge, the colour had returned to Euhemia's cheeks. Lou had to wonder if it wasn't the restriction of the hospital making her sick.

Lou left Cass in charge of the store under the pretense of running errands for Euphemia, which would allow her to visit Phillip's house when he wasn't home. Cass seemed happy for the opportunity to spend time in the store alone. Lou had given her specific tasks to complete, to keep her busy, and Lou was still pleasantly surprised at how much she enjoyed having a companion during working hours.

The night before, Lou had left Cass in the store while she drove Euphemia home from the hospital. Cass was supposed to lock up and head home by the time Lou returned to the store, but Cass was sitting behind the register when Lou turned her key in the door and knocked the snow from her boots against the wall.

"Cass, you startled me. I didn't expect you to be here so late. Everything okay?"

Cass didn't have her headphones in, and her bangs were pulled back from her face with a black barrette.

"I wanted to be here when you got back, because I need to talk to you about something," Cass said. "Al came in and asked about the chair you're fixing for him, and I didn't know where you'd put it, so I had a look around. I didn't know the back room was off limits, I just figured the door was jammed, so I picked the lock."

Lou grabbed a stool by the wooden seat, and pulled it over so that she could sit in front of Cass. She braced herself for what might come next, not totally surprised. It was only a matter of time before the girl found out; but maybe she hadn't found the keys.

"Are you living here?" Cass asked.

"Yes, but it's only temporary. I never meant for anyone to find out."

"Why didn't you tell me?"

"I didn't want anyone to know. Like I said, it's temporary. I never planned to live here long enough for anyone to need to know."

"But why? Don't you have your parents' house?"

Lou took a deep breath. "I do," she said, "but I don't know if I'm ready to live in it yet."

"Why not?"

Lou took a moment to think about the question; she'd never articulated why she couldn't go back; it was just a gut feeling.

"I know that I'll walk in and it'll look like home. It might even still smell like home. And I'm not ready to know that my home doesn't exist anymore. It can't, because the people that made it home are gone and they aren't coming back."

Cass nodded, and even though she was young, Lou had a feeling she understood.

"Louise, you know you could come and stay with my family, right? If people knew you were living here, you'd be invited to stay anywhere."

"I know." Lou waited a moment to decide what she wanted to say next. "I'm just learning to be by myself, is all. I don't want to do that with too many other people around."

Cass leaned over the cash register and placed a hand over top of Lou's.

"I know I can't imagine what you've been going through. But I'm here, you know? This is the best job I've ever had. I'd love to own a place like this someday. I want to go to university and do other things first, but this is my dream. I guess what I'm trying to say is that I know your secret, but I hope you'll let me stay anyway. I like it here."

Lou didn't know what to say and waited out a long silence before stammering, "I'd love it if you stayed."

Even after the conversation with Cass, Lou had taken to keeping her stash of keys in her bag at all times, which meant that her shoulder was beginning to ache from the weight. Eventually, she'd feel the ache traversing her shoulder and up to the top of her head if she didn't begin to leave some of the keys behind. If Cass could pick the lock to the back room, her secrets weren't safe there anymore.

*****

Lou didn't know much about Phillip and his metal detector despite both having lived in Snowton all their lives. She only knew that Phillip was a detectorist who had yet to uncover his big, life-changing find. He told stories at the pub about detectorists who had discovered buried treasure, decaying fingers that still wore valuable rings, Bronze Age axe heads, or pieces of meteors. So far, the most impressive item that Phillip had unearthed was a small metal figurine of Jesus that he kept in his coat pocket. He would pull it out and show it off at every opportunity, prompted or not.

Since there was no bell, just an antique doorknocker that looked like it belonged on a gothic mansion, Lou knocked on the door. She waited for sounds to emanate from inside. She didn't expect him to answer the door, even if he was at home, because Phillip considered himself 'antisocial.' When she knocked again and was met with silence, she took the key from her pocket, looked behind her to ensure no one was around, and slipped the key in the lock. The key caught—the mechanism seemed jammed in some way. Lou wiggled the key back and forth, knowing that every moment she spent wrestling with the lock was a moment closer to being caught. She willed her palms not to sweat so that she could keep her grip as she gave the key one final twist. There was a sharp crack and the lock released. She was in.

Closing the door behind her, she was taken aback by the sheer volume of objects that Phillip had stuffed into such a small space. Each wall was lined with shelves and each shelf was stacked with labelled storage containers. *PAPERWORK. COINS. ELECTRONICS. BOOKMARKS. WATCHES. NEWSPAPERS. EPHEMERA.* When she opened the container nearest to her, labelled *NEWSPAPERS*, she found copies of the town paper dating back to the forties. The next container was filled to the brim with Canadian collector coins, with poppies, birth stones, ferrets, tulips, and so on emblazoned into the metal. Another container held earbuds and headphones. When she lifted the lid of the last container on that shelf, she wasn't surprised to find it filled with hundreds of watches—children's watches, antiques, modern watches with beeping alarms, all issuing a cacophonic ticking. One watch to the right of the pile caught her eye: a large gold-faced watch with an engraving of a keyhole at the twelve o'clock mark. She recognized it because it had been her birthday gift to Edward the year before her parents died, but he'd lost it only a month after receiving it. So, Phillip's magpie-like obsession with collecting did not stop at coins and newspapers, and he was clearly not above theft. She felt indignant at first and then remembered that she had her own secrets. And she still had a task to complete. She hadn't found the necklace, yet.

Lou walked to the kitchen and saw a scrabble board on the table. She had a momentary flash of panic that he was home with company, but on second glance, it seemed he was playing by himself. Only one set of letters was set out, and beside the board was one cup of coffee that had developed a layer of scum around the surface. She let out a sigh of relief at the state of the coffee cup, which showed that he'd likely been away from the game for hours if not days. She looked at the letters and words he'd played.

cart
cruel
baculum
slick
sway
cyanide
billbug
lover
plug
recluse
chartreuse
actuarian
indigo
over
rust
locksmith
here

The words that first jumped out at her were *locksmith* and *indigo*. She wondered if they could have anything to do with her and her situation, or if she was reading too much into them. Then, she considered the triple word score he'd won for *cyanide*. If he had killed Isabella, was that how he'd done it? If he hadn't, did he know something about who had?

Euphemia had been right: Phillip *was* like a magpie, glittering bits all through his house reflecting the sunlight. While he'd organized most of his treasures in storage containers, the ones that caught and refracted the sunlight were tucked into corners, between books, behind vases. One such treasure was a hand painted Christmas ornament; another was a necklace (but not the one she was looking for). Between his couch and the wall sat an antique bar cart with crystal tumblers and a half-full bottle of whiskey. She was inspecting the bar cart and the ice bucket when she heard a floorboard creak and a voice call out, "Hello?"

Lou realized with a warm, uncomfortable heat in her stomach, that she had closed but hadn't locked the door behind her.

"Phillip? Are you home?"

Looking around, she decided that her best option was to hide behind the couch. She couldn't place the voice that rang through the house. It was female, so it wasn't Phillip, but everyone in town knew Lou. She rolled the bar cart further behind the couch as quietly as she could and crouched down in the opening between the two.

"Phillip? The door was unlocked, I just wanted to see if you were all right."

Lou held her breath and placed her hand over her mouth so that she wouldn't make a sound. A shadow fell across the couch and Lou waited before looking up, desperate for a few more moments of peace before her life would be ruined more than she'd already ruined it.

"Sloppy work, Louise. Really sloppy." Euphemia peeked her head above the couch, and Lou's body shuddered from her sudden exhalation.

"What the hell are you doing here? You scared the shit out of me."

"That was the intention. This is some of the spottiest work I've encountered."

Lou struggled for breath. She felt as though her heart had stopped and restarted in the span of ten seconds. "That doesn't give you the right to scare me like that."

"It gives me every right—you didn't even lock the door behind you! Careless, Louise, really careless."

Louise sputtered in reply, because her heart still felt like it would charge out of her chest.

Euphemia's eyes were like steely blue windows. "You have to do better."

"I don't want to do better. I don't want more of this—breaking and entering. I'm done."

"Take some deep breaths, Louise. I need you to be in better shape for the Higgins' house."

"Didn't you hear me? I said I'm done."

"I heard you perfectly well, I'm not deaf. To be frank, quitting is not an option for you. Go back to your store, rest up, and be ready for the next one in a few days. I'll finish up here." She held out her hand, into which Lou placed the housekey.

Lou grabbed her coat from where she'd left it on the floor, fastened the buckles on her winter boots, and opened the front door. As she exited, she didn't look around to make sure the area was clear, but she did resist an urge to slam the door behind her. She didn't feel the thrill or the confidence at having gotten away with something. This time, she meant what she said. She'd had enough.

CHAPTER 16

Lou was thankful when she found herself walking through
the metal gates of the Snowton cemetery. She hadn't planned
to walk to the cemetery, but she recognized that something
like a gravitational pull guided her body toward the front gate;
she had little choice in the matter. The exercise chums weren't
around, she didn't hear a single bird call, and the wind had
finally relented for long enough that she could stand up straight
and walk forward without being pushed backwards. She didn't
have news to share—she simply picked pinecones off the path,
cleared snow from the tops of headstones, and sat against her
parents' stones with their gentle pressure on her back.

She thought of cemeteries she'd seen in books and
magazines, cemeteries that were far more beautiful and better
maintained than the Snowton Cemetery, but she couldn't
imagine that they would yield the same atmosphere of safety or
comfort. She'd read that in London, Highgate cemetery housed
fifty-three thousand graves and had an award-winning Head
Gardener. Glasnevin cemetery in Dublin had a museum and
covered one hundred and twenty-four acres. But still, Snowton
was where Lou belonged. And in her shabby, local, one hundred
and fifty plot-cemetery, Lou began to cry.

CHAPTER 17

Lou tried to understand why she felt so angry. She hadn't locked the door behind her at Phillip's house, which *was* truly careless, but the odds of someone trying the door handle at the exact moment she was housebreaking were so slim. And yet. She didn't know why she felt like Euphemia had taken something away from her. She hadn't wanted any of this in the first place; it should have been a relief to have been caught by Euphemia—to show that she wasn't cut out for this subterfuge and to extricate herself from the whole situation.

The problem, in Lou's eyes anyway, was that she was cut out for this. She had never felt as calm as when she was sliding a key that she had no right to own into a lock that wasn't hers. Her palms stopped sweating; her heart rate slowed to what she imagined was an optimal pace. Her mind was clear—she felt capable. If Euphemia hadn't caught her with the door unlocked, that feeling might never have gone away, and Lou could have held onto it for a little bit longer.

She'd had enough of Euphemia telling her what to do, but perhaps it was time to make some decisions for herself. She couldn't deny that she loved the thrill. After the argument with Euphemia, she *needed* the thrill.

*****

On Tuesday evenings, Eve and Al drove to Calgary to see a discount movie. She still called it 'Toonie Tuesday,' even though the price hadn't been a toonie since the nineties. Al and Eve alternated who chose the movie each week—they'd been doing this since Al was a young boy. This meant that the house would be empty for at least a couple of hours.

Lou slid the key into the lock, felt the subtle vibration as the pins tumbled against the key blade, and the door to their home inched open as if to welcome her inside. She had been in their home many times, mostly to pick up Stuart, but Eve always invited her in for tea, and they'd chat for hours while the boys played video games in the next room. Lou felt bold, so she put some water in the electric kettle and helped herself to a bag of orange pekoe from the glass jar on the counter and a Delfts Blue mug from the cupboard above the sink. She would wash everything before she made her exit, and they would never know she'd been there.

Lou envied the south-facing window, where Eve's potted succulents basked in the sun. Any plant Lou tried to grow shrivelled and died within a week; she either overwatered when she was supposed to water infrequently, or she underwatered a plant that needed constant moisture. There was no point in trying to grow plants in the hardware store. She figured the sawdust, paint thinner, bits of spackling, and various compounds would stifle any plant life. If that weren't enough, the lack of light certainly wouldn't help.

Lou poured the kettle and took her tea black so that she wouldn't need to touch Eve's milk and sugar; the risk of spilling or leaving a trace of her visit was too high. She sat down at the kitchen table with her tea, took a first sip, and pretended for a moment that this was her kitchen. Those were her plants on the windowsill—her aloe plant she'd nurtured, her bamboo that curled around a popsicle stick. She pretended until a photograph on the fridge caught her eye. It was tattered at one end, and a blue streak ran down the middle as though it had been printed on an inkjet printer with just barely enough ink remaining: Al and Eve dressed as pumpkins for Halloween. They each had green hats on their heads that were meant to be pumpkin stems. Lou remembered that year distinctly; the twins were ten, and she'd dressed Stuart as the Tin Man from *The Wizard of Oz*. He hoped his sister might join him and choose a costume that was at least thematically related. Instead, Molly decided to be a piece of pizza. She wore all black, and Lou crafted the front and back of the pizza slice out of cardboard, which fastened over her shoulders with suspenders. Molly hadn't required too much else for decoration, but Stuart insisted she cover every bare inch of his skin in silver face paint. At one point, Lou wondered if the paint might be toxic in large quantities, but she didn't have time to wonder for long. She and the kids were going out trick or treating with Al and Eve in fifteen minutes. Edward was supposed to have been home an hour earlier to help. Lou got the kids bundled in winter coats first, since Halloween in Snowton always included snowsuits. The seams of Stuart's costume were stretched to their limit with his ski pants beneath, but she would rather he be a little tight than frostbitten. Molly's was easier. She simply tugged the snow pants onto her legs and zipped up her jacket, then lowered the cardboard pizza pieces over her shoulders.

"Mom, it's too tight with my snowsuit, I can't breathe," Stuart said.

"You can too breathe, dear. It's this or freezing to death, your choice."

"I think I'd rather freeze."

"You know, I said your choice, but I didn't really mean it. Now come on, zip up. You'll feel better once we get outside."

"Where's daddy?" Molly asked.

Lou looked at her watch. "It looks like he's a little late."

"Did he forget it's Halloween?"

"I reminded him this morning," Stuart said.

At that moment, Lou heard a key in the front door, saw the deadbolt turn ninety degrees, and Edward entered the foyer with a blanketed bundle in his arms.

"Sorry I'm late."

"Daddy! We were going to leave without you," Molly was already getting good at punishing him.

"You are years late," Lou muttered under her breath when Edward leaned over and kissed her on the cheek.

"I had to stop and pick somebody up."

"What are you talking about?"

Edward unwrapped the blanket to reveal a pitch-black kitten with blue eyes and white whiskers. And just like that, all was forgiven in her children's eyes. Edward had brought them this small bundle, and they loved him for it.

*****

Lou hadn't noticed, but at some point, she'd crossed the room and taken the photo from the fridge. She shook the memories away by putting the photo back beneath the magnet, exactly as she'd found it. She sipped the last of her black tea, which had gone cold, washed her cup in the sink, and did a visual sweep of the kitchen to make sure she hadn't left anything behind or out of place. She didn't search for Isabella's necklace; Eve's house wasn't on the hit list. She felt no thrill or excitement. A feeling like acid was rising in the back of her throat. She knew where her next visit needed to be.

CHAPTER 18

Lou thought she'd heard every story Snowton had to offer.
She knew about the midwife responsible for catching most of
the babies born between 1940 and 1995. Lou knew about the
time a convicted criminal had hitchhiked his way to town,
and, once he arrived, rented Frank Blake's spare bedroom
for two months before he was found and returned to prison.
She knew about the time a human statue took up residence in
Snowton—appearing with no warning, standing motionless on
Main Street for one week, and disappearing with no warning.
Lou knew about the man who collected moths, the hailstorm
of '05, the postal worker's strike, the sinkhole. She knew that
her grandfather (who had died before she was born) had told
Lou's mother to take their cat's newborn kittens, put them in
a bag, and put the bag in the river. Lou's mother told her that
she'd put the kittens in a paper bag, so the kittens swam in all
directions. Her mother never said what happened next.

Lou had heard these stories, some of which she knew could
not be true. But she carried them around inside of her like
strawberry seeds—they took root until they became part of her.

CHAPTER 19

Lou waited in her own car, parked comfortably down the street, until she was sure theirs had rounded the corner at the end of the block. She lingered a few more moments, just to make sure they wouldn't turn the car around if the kids had forgotten anything. She walked up the familiar drive. Ice patches were spreading from the downspout; it happened every year with the freeze and thaw, but it seemed that Edward hadn't put any ice melt down this year. She had an image of their mail carrier launching down the drive while trying to deliver their bills. She'd make sure to put some down before she left. She made her way to the front door, arms out to the side for balance, and opened the door with the only key that was rightfully hers. She was careful to knock the snow and slush off her boots before coming in—she didn't want to leave any trace of her visit. The lock opened smoothly, and she stepped inside, removing her boots on the hooked rug she'd bought at a Christmas market in Calgary.

Lou stood in the entryway and took stock of her old home: the clock on the wall with a jar of jam on the end of the minute hand and a tub of honey on the hours. The painting of a bumblebee hive Molly had done. The stack of dishes in the sink because the dishwasher was still broken (she'd meant to fix it before she left, but then decided not to). The beige cat bed on the ottoman, even though Magician no longer lived there. Lou moved from the entryway into the living room to the kitchen to her old bedroom, and, finally, she stopped in Stuart and Molly's bedrooms. In Stuart's she found a small mountain of homework on his desk, a math test with a score of ninety-eight percent, and a stack of novels on his end table. Stuart had never been a big reader, but from the bookstack, it looked as though he might be taking an interest in science fiction. In Molly's room, she discovered that the walls were a different shade from when she'd left (Rainwater P450-3, she thought). The teddy bears and other stuffed animals that used to line her shelves were gone and, instead, Molly had placed photo frames—some of them empty, some of them with photos of her friends, and one with a photo of her and Lou together. Edward had taken the shot of the two of them after a trip to Sylvan Lake. They had sand in their hair and teeth and blazing sunburnt blotches on their noses.

Lou kneeled beside Molly's bed first, then Stuart's, and put her face into their pillows, breathing in their smells. In her mind, she imagined they were sleeping as children and she was kissing their foreheads while trying not to wake them. Before she left, she took the bag of ice melt from the garage and sprinkled it down the drive, leaving a watery blue trail in her wake.

CHAPTER 20

A few days later, and against her better judgment, Lou walked up the drive to the Higgins' house with Euphemia at her side. Euphemia had insisted she come along so that they wouldn't have a repeat of the situation at Phillip's house. Euphemia wore black leggings with red rain boots and a sweater that looked like a cape with bat sleeves. Her cane made a slow tapping sound when it touched the icy pavement. Lou wore what she always wore: jeans that were a size and a half too large, winter boots, and a pullover fleece that had once belonged to her husband. Euphemia munched from a bag of Hobnobs she held in her free hand.

Euphemia had been right about the garden gnomes. They lined the driveway on either side, and Lou felt a chill at the gaze of their cold, painted eyes. The snow from early February had melted during a Chinook—without snowcaps the gnomes seemed even more desolate, almost menacing. Their feet were planted in the earth, but their heads had faded in the sun, and they were surrounded by brown dirt and gravel.

"The Higgins couple has got to be hiding something." Euphemia said as she bumped one of the gnomes with the tip of her rain boot. "It's not *natural* to have this many gnomes."

The Hobnobs had been closed with a crumb covered piece of tape and slipped into Lou's handbag. She knew there would be crumbs hiding in every crevasse and seam.

"Let's get inside the house first. We can look at the gnomes later."

"Did you know that garden gnomes were originally called *Gartenzwerge*? It's German for Garden Dwarf."

"Can we *please* discuss gnomes later? I want to get inside."

"I think we should liberate one. She has so many, she wouldn't notice if one took a walk."

In truth, Lou didn't want the gnomes' eyes on her any longer than necessary, and the more time she and Euphemia spent in the driveway, the more suspect they became.

At the front door, Euphemia rang the bell, and Lou looked behind them. No one was coming up the drive, but the gnomes' beady eyes were fixed on her. When they heard nothing inside the house, and no one came to answer the door, Lou slid the small silver key into the lock and turned it.

"The coast looks clear," she whispered as she peeked her head around the doorframe.

"Of course it's clear. They're out at marriage counselling."

They both entered, and Louise made a show of locking the front door behind them. There was nothing remarkable about the house except for its paint job, a colour that reminded Lou of the 'Mayonnaise' paint chips in the store. Neither Louise nor Euphemia could find anything amiss. It took half the time with the two of them searching, but they met back at the front door empty-handed. Lou couldn't understand why, but Euphemia was desperate to return to the garden gnomes. After locking the door behind them and stepping back outside, Euphemia reached for a garden gnome that was fatter than the others, removed the glove from her hand, and put it inside the ceramic cavity through the hole in the bottom.

"There's something in here, but it won't budge."

Euphemia twisted her hand, gave one last tug and as she withdrew her hand from the gnome, they both saw that she held a second, smaller gnome. It had been hidden inside the first.

"These people are crazy. Who needs this many garden gnomes?" Euphemia's brow furrowed.

"What did you expect to find?"

"The necklace, money, drugs—anything other than more goddamn garden gnomes."

Euphemia tucked both the chubby gnome and his smaller companion under her arm and walked to the car. Lou followed a few feet behind. Their work at the Higgins house was done, and it had yielded nothing.

They visited Mark and Beth Dull's house the same day. Their home was perfectly clean, the mark of two adults with ample income and no children. The walls were painted a pleasant light yellow (Cream #FFDD0, if Lou wasn't mistaken).

As they entered the house, Lou mulled over what Beth had said about Euphemia at the hospital.

Batty old lady.

Hemlock tea.

For the first time, Lou wondered if Euphemia could have killed Isabella. Lou allowed herself to think through the question in its complexity. She wondered if these break-ins were a façade—if Euphemia had planted the necklace on someone in an attempt to frame them.

The last person on their list was Edward. Lou didn't want him in her life, but she didn't want him to be accused of murder, either. She felt more guarded than usual as she watched Euphemia pull books that were expertly alphabetized off the shelf and check the spaces behind.

"Beth used to come around to my house quite often," Euphemia said as she continued to check the bookshelves.

"Did she really?" Lou found this difficult to believe.

"I taught her how to knit after her miscarriage. She hadn't even told anyone she was pregnant. I knew, of course."

"How did you know?"

"I have my ways."

"But at the hospital, she said—" Euphemia tucked one of the books under her arm.

"Did she say something nasty about me?"

Lou paused before she answered. "She called you a 'batty old lady.'"

"She wouldn't be the first, and I'm quite certain she won't be the last."

"Doesn't that bother you?"

"Not in the slightest."

"But how? How do you let something like that go?" Lou was thinking of the rumours that circulated about her parents' deaths, the insinuations she'd heard. She'd tried to keep them from getting under her skin—to stay at a surface level with everyone so that she wouldn't be hurt by the remarks.

"Well, *you* don't think I'm a batty old lady, and *I* don't think I am, and two good opinions are quite enough for me." She stopped pulling books, and turned to face Lou.

Lou couldn't bring herself to ask, but she wondered who Euphemia's sources were. How could she possibly know so much? She secretly wondered if Euphemia knew anything about her parents. If she'd known about Beth's miscarriage, and Bart's writer's block, that Mark and Beth were at marriage counselling, maybe her sources could have told her what happened that day in her parents' house. But Lou knew that she wasn't ready to find out for sure that she'd been wrong or that she'd failed as a daughter. She would rather live with the unknown ache of wondering than be certain.

After a thorough search of the house, the pair left the way they came, empty-handed; all they had to show for their day's work were the garden gnomes that Euphemia had buckled into the back seat of the car.

CHAPTER 21

Euphemia was back in the hospital two days after the break-in at the Dull's house, with pain in the side of her chest. This meant she could invite Frank to visit her at the hospital and guarantee he would be out for the entirety of Lou's break-in. Before she gave Lou the all clear, Euphemia had to find out if anyone was living with him.

Although Lou didn't understand the appeal herself, Frank was a serial dater. He'd come into the hardware store after each break-up to get a new key cut for the next one. Luckily, Frank Blake was between partners, and he never seemed to care that his ex-partners took their keys with them when they left, which made Lou feel slightly better about entering his home uninvited. She had a key when she wasn't supposed to, but so did every person that Frank had ever dated.

Euphemia felt confident that she could keep Frank at the hospital for an hour, which would give Lou plenty of time to get in, investigate, and escape without leaving a trace. Lou had the logistics covered by this point: park a few blocks away, take a cursory glance up and down the street, walk briskly up the driveway, ring the doorbell, take another swift check behind her, put the key in the lock with a satisfying twist, and she was in. She worried that she'd left footprints in the Dull's house, so she'd ordered a shipment of boot covers into the store and brought a few with her to Frank's.

Since Lou and Euphemia had begun their break-ins, Lou had noticed a change in the atmosphere around Snowton. Folks were beginning to notice that something was amiss. They may not have known what exactly was wrong, but there was a shift to the balance in their town. There were more road accidents (nothing fatal, only fender benders), people walked out of grocery stores and forgot to pay for the roll of paper towels they'd stashed on the bottom rung of the cart, they pushed doors that they knew they should pull, and more people were in the emergency room because of household accidents: burns, cuts, and other mishaps. They were distracted and preoccupied, but if you asked them what the matter was, they probably wouldn't be able to tell you. Still, something was amiss in Snowton, and everyone could feel it.

While this wasn't what she'd envisioned for herself, Lou couldn't stop the small thrill that seeped into her bones in the moments before entering the house. Frank's house was cleaner than the Dulls'—his shoes were placed neatly on a rack, and everything seemed in the right place. In theory, she thought, this would make it easier for her to notice if something was out of place. She began in the living room, which was directly off the main entryway, and then went into the kitchen, where there were no dirty dishes, no crumbs on the counter, and no half-drunk cups of coffee cooling on the stove. Remembering that Frank had been willing to put a raw turkey over his face for a laugh, she was surprised he could be so neat. She'd expected markers of bachelordom since he was living alone: beer cans in the sink, pizza boxes atop the black garbage bin because they were too large to fit inside, dirty socks tucked underneath the couch cushions.

Lou felt a flutter in her chest that she hadn't expected. She felt a gut reaction to this house—it was too clean. Which made it look like he had something to hide. She had a feeling this nightmare could soon be over.

She opened his fridge, casually checked his garbage cans (which were almost empty, apart from the odd used tissue), and decided that since the house was so clean, she would need to think more methodically. She looked for oddities in the spacing of items, anything that was off centre or that felt different. She ran her hands along the walls to grope for bumps or secret compartments and, eventually, she came upon a locked door that she assumed led to the basement.

She tried the front door key, but it didn't fit. It was a long shot, but over ten minutes, she tried a third of the other keys on her carabiner.

Louise yanked a screwdriver from the belt of her jeans (she'd taken to carrying tools around for a situation just like this) and began removing the screws from the doorknob. It was painstakingly slow work given the circumstances, but she knew she was onto something. One by one, the screws came loose, and she had enough space between the doorframe and the knob to insert her screwdriver and apply pressure until she felt the bolt pop out of place and she could unlock the door.

From where she stood in the doorway, she was looking down a darkened stairway that led around a corner into blackness. She tried not to imagine what she might find down there. The stairs creaked as she descended, and the smell was a stark contrast to the rest of the house: musty, dirty, and dank. Upon rounding the corner, she saw a large freezer with an industrial-sized plug connected to an outlet on the other side of the room. Every horror story she'd ever heard about bodies in freezers, or parts of bodies wrapped in plastic, flickered in her brain, and for a moment, she wanted to turn back, wanted to leave without replacing the screws on the door, and pretend that she'd never seen anything. She reminded herself that this whole ordeal was almost over, but she needed to look in the freezer. She couldn't just walk away.

She jumped when her phone vibrated in her pocket. As she accepted the call, she heard Euphemia say, "He just left. I couldn't keep him any longer."

"Damn. Is he on foot or driving?"

"On foot. My guess is you've got fifteen minutes before he comes through the front door."

"Okay. Listen, I might have found something important."

"He's in the elevator now, and I won't be far behind him."

"What do you mean?"

"I'm breaking out. We don't have time to waste, Louise," Euphemia hung up.

She was less than arms-length away from the freezer. She propped her fingers beneath the vacuum-sealed lid, unsure of how heavy it would be or how quickly it would open. She lifted the lid with her eyes shut, only opening them when the lid was fully raised.

Her stomach sank, partly from relief that she hadn't found a hand, or a full set of human teeth, or worse, a whole body, but then she couldn't help feeling disappointment. The freezer was full of small packages wrapped in tinfoil, roughly the size of individual chicken breasts. It wasn't over. They hadn't found the killer.

With only a few minutes to fix the door and make her retreat, Lou was about to close the freezer when she realized that the packages were all identical in size. She picked one up from the top of the stack and gingerly peeled back the foil the way she might pluck petals from a flower. Her fingers didn't touch frozen meat as she'd expected, but paper. Inside the foil was a stack of twenty-dollar bills. She reached for another package. By the time she'd opened ten more packages, she estimated that she'd counted over five thousand dollars. After clearing enough of the packages from the freezer, she could see a much smaller one tucked into the back corner and her heart began to race.

As she reached down to pick it up, she heard a key in the lock upstairs, Frank must have run home from the hospital— the sound of boots knocking winter slush onto the carpet, followed by a whistle which reminded her of a song her father used to hum. Lou began searching the room for a window, a closet, something she could hide in or use to make an escape. It was only a matter of time before Frank would spot the open door, the loose screws on the floor, and hear her rummaging around downstairs. She listened intently, hoping to pinpoint where in the house he might be.

Then, she heard a sound she'd never expected would make her so happy. An upstairs door shutting followed by the tinkling sound of urination. She put the small tin foil package in the pocket of her jeans and took the stairs as quietly as she could, while listening for the flush which would signal that it was too late and she'd been caught. She tiptoed by the bathroom door with all of the lightness she could muster, through the kitchen and back into the entryway where she unlocked the door, closed it behind her and locked it. If he was going to run after her, she needed the extra seconds it would take for Frank to open the door. Only then did she release the breath she'd been holding as she tried to calm her shaking hands.

Euphemia came up the drive to meet Lou, her eyes wide with concern as she latched the front gate behind her and saw the notice taped to the wood.

Emergency town hall meeting to address recent break-ins.
Tonight, 8 PM.
ALL are encouraged to attend.

Euphemia and Lou walked three blocks without speaking, when Lou stopped.

She took the ball of tin foil from her pocket, unwrapped it and wordlessly held it up for Euphemia to examine. Isabella's blue necklace was nestled inside.

CHAPTER 22

At the meeting, Lou had difficulty holding her pen, because her hands were sweating. She tried her best to look neutral in times of stress, but she was certain she looked suspicious. She remembered when she was ten, a shopkeeper in Calgary had accused her of shoplifting when she'd only been carrying an item around the store before buying it. She'd been so worried about looking like she was shoplifting that she had unintentionally made herself look suspicious, and she worried she was doing the same in the meeting.

Now, she tried to relax her eyebrows and drop her jaw so that it wasn't clenched quite so tight. She hoped that as minute-taker she might disappear into the background. No one would wonder why she didn't speak up or express an interest in what was being discussed. They knew she had a job to do. She'd always taken meeting minutes, but she had never been so invested in a meeting before. From her seat, she could see everyone in attendance, Edward, Euphemia, the owners of every house she'd entered, and Frank Blake, who looked paler than normal, as well as a few others who probably had no vested interest, but wouldn't turn down an opportunity to hear local gossip.

When they'd unwrapped the necklace down the street from Frank's house, Euphemia and Lou had looked up at each other, clearly experiencing different emotions. Euphemia looked triumphant. Lou not only felt relief that it was over, but also some disappointment she couldn't place. She didn't need to break into more houses, but she was also strangely comforted by the knowledge that Edward hadn't stolen the necklace. He sat at the back of the room and was blissfully unaware that he'd ever been suspected of theft, or worse, murder.

At the meeting, Euphemia voiced as much concern as the real victims of break-ins and even mentioned that she'd been burgled. Lou hoped that Euphemia would have her back, and that they'd both been diligent enough to cover their tracks.

She took the minutes, but she didn't process any of it.

What proof do you have?

Was anything taken?

Why weren't you home?

Did you leave your door unlocked?

Who do you think it was?

Who could possibly break into our homes without breaking any windows or doors?

Suddenly, an explanation for the fog of confusion that had surrounded Snowton for weeks: their homes and security had been compromised. They'd all known something was off. They knew the kettle was slightly to the left of where it sat when they returned home. There hadn't been *that* many boot prints on the entryway mat, had there? Could the cat really have knocked over a vase? *Anna Karenina* was to the right of *Wuthering Heights*, wasn't it?

These questions swarmed through their minds, and just when it seemed they might circle around to Lou as a suspect, Euphemia stood up and walked over to Frank Blake, tapped him on the shoulder, and ushered him to the back of the room. No one seemed to notice Frank and Euphemia's departure, and the meeting continued without them. Lou watched them talking at the back of the room, wishing that she could read lips. Frank ran a hand through his hair before sitting down in a nearby chair with his head bowed. She must be blackmailing him. He was about to confess to the murder. Lou found that she wanted to jump out of her chair, but she forced herself to remain seated.

Euphemia returned to her seat and left Frank at the back of the room. He was no longer pale, but ghostly. A few moments later, he got up, slowly stood to his full height, and left the community hall—no confession, no declaration, no resolution.

Euphemia walked to the front of the room, went up to Randy, the chair, and whispered something in his ear. Within moments, the meeting was adjourned, and the townsfolk confusedly began to trickle out of the hall, without any final judgement about the break-ins. Lou caught Euphemia by the arm as the others milled around the entrance of the community hall. She didn't say anything; she simply stared, knowing that Euphemia would know the question that was on her lips.

"Frank is going to meet us at my house, and then I think I ought to go back to the hospital. I suppose they're looking for me," was all she said.

"Is it safe for us to be alone with him? He killed Isabella. What if he's planning the same for us?"

Euphemia shook her head and smiled, "He's harmless enough."

They walked in silence, and when they arrived at Euphemia's front door, Frank was waiting outside, sheepish, his hands tucked into his coat pockets. Lou noticed that a small vein in the side of his neck was more noticeable than usual; she hoped he wouldn't have a heart attack from the stress. She wanted him alive, because she and Euphemia needed answers.

Euphemia laughed and said, "Shall I unlock the door, or should you?" with a slight shiver at the end of her question. The temperature had dropped at least ten degrees in the time they'd been in the meeting.

As Euphemia turned the key, Lou smelled the familiar scent of earth and sprouts and growth that emanated from the house.

Once the door was shut, they could speak freely. Questions began to pour out of Lou like a running tap. She had planned to let Euphemia take the lead, but she couldn't help herself once they were behind closed doors.

"You killed Isabella. Was it her money in your freezer? Did you kill her for the money?"

Euphemia spoke before Frank could. "No, yes, and, fortunately, no, I don't think so." Euphemia gestured at Lou and Frank to sit down and take off their coats and scarves.

In that moment, Frank looked as if he wanted to be anywhere else. He continued to shiver even though Euphemia's living room was warm and moist with plant life.

She handed Frank a glass and poured him a large amount of red wine.

"Frank, would you like to start?" Her opening reminded Lou of a support group meeting. She'd only been to one in Calgary after her parents' death, and she vowed never to attend another. The meeting was for those recently divorced or bereaved. She hadn't lost her husband in a car accident; he hadn't left her for someone else—she had lost her parents. She received little sympathy from the other group members, because parents were supposed to die, but spouses were not.

Frank made no motions to speak, and so Euphemia began.

"Isabella never told me that she had children before she came to Snowton, and that one of her daughters was a fling of Frank's." She tipped her head in his direction as if willing him to step up and take over.

Frank took a large swig of wine, emptying his glass, and holding it out to Euphemia for a refill. Once he had a full glass, he took over the conversation.

"We have a son together," he paused and ran a hand through his salt and pepper hair. "He lives in Calgary with his mother, Tabatha. We're not on good terms." Frank's voice shook a little, and he cleared his throat before continuing. "I've made some bad decisions with money. I gambled, I borrowed—I thought I knew what I was doing." He took a long drink of his second glass of wine.

"Tabatha told him that her mother's health was failing. He went to Isabella and asked her for money. He thought she might be generous, since she wouldn't need the money for too much longer." Euphemia didn't try to hide the disdain in her voice; she wanted Frank to hear every drop of it.

"She told me to get a job. She told me that I'd always been a lazy bum, and that she wished her daughter had never met me. She said the only good I'd ever done was bringing her grandson into the world, but that was it. I was going to leave empty-handed, but then she fell asleep."

Euphemia shook her head. "I'd warned her about falling asleep with company over. She'd done it with me before, but then, I had her best interests at heart, unlike Frank."

"I undid the clasp of her necklace while she was sleeping, and I slid it into my pocket. I was going to sell it online. Then, I scavenged her house for anything of value. I took money from her cashbox and all of the bills she kept wrapped in tin foil in her freezer. But I swear she was healthy when I left. She was asleep, but she was alive and breathing. I didn't know she was going to die later that day, and as soon as I heard, I ran to her house to put everything back, but then it was crawling with people. You," he looked to Euphemia, "were watching everyone like a vulture. There was nothing I could do. So, I hid everything in my house, and I hoped that no one would ever have to know what I'd done. But I didn't kill her. I promise you, I'm not a killer." He downed the last of his wine and tried to take deep breaths. Lou saw a drop of sweat beading against his forehead and trickling down the side of his face.

"Frank and I had a fruitful discussion at the meeting, and I believe we have reached an agreement. He agrees not to blab about our break-ins and we agree not to divulge his thievery."

Frank nodded vigorously, then put his head in his hands.

Lou tapped Euphemia on the shoulder and tilted her head toward the kitchen; Euphemia steadied herself on Lou's arm as she stood, and the two shuffled through the doorframe.

"So, you believe him? You think Isabella died of natural causes?" Lou whispered.

"I can't say for sure," Euphemia leaned back against the wall, "but I tell you, I never thought I'd be solving murders at my age—let alone murders that may not have happened."

"You believe him. I'm not entirely convinced."

"That may be something we have to learn to live with."

Frank coughed from the other room as if to remind them he was still there and could hear their conversation. Lou came back out from the kitchen with a finger pointed at him; her pointer finger had a slight bend at the top knuckle from an old woodworking injury. It was clear enough to Frank that she was angry.

"How can we be sure you'll keep your word?"

Before Frank could speak, Euphemia placed a hand on Lou's shoulder.

"Frank is not a stupid man. He's an irresponsible one, for sure, but not stupid. He knows how it will look if he's found with wads of cash in his freezer, not to mention Isabella's necklace. I'm simply going to remind him, every once in a while, that I could give him a reputation as a thief, as a murderer, or as neither." She looked at him and smiled gently as she spoke. Her facial expressions and her words did not match, and Frank clearly picked up on the discrepancy.

He knew the position he was in, and that if Euphemia had a plan for him, he would go along without resistance.

"You may go, Frank. And remember your promise."

Lou had never seen him so eager to leave. She wondered if he, too, was overwhelmed by the smell of plant life, or if he simply wanted to get home and wipe away any trace of his mistake. He practically ran out the door without closing it behind him, and he did not look back.

Lou remembered the first break-in, and the injury that caused everything that followed. She still had the black toenail as a reminder of how it all began. She watched his retreating figure under the light of the streetlamps and closed the door. She sank down in a chair and felt relief that they'd reached an agreement. He couldn't speak about their break-ins without implicating himself. They had a pact that couldn't be broken.

"So, what do we do now?" Lou asked.

"What do you mean?"

"What's our next step?"

"We're done, Lou. This mystery has been put to rest. Now we go on living."

Lou was suddenly disappointed with everything, a feeling she neither had expected nor understood. Ever since this ordeal had begun, she'd wanted it to be over, but she was unable to prevent the sweeping sense of placelessness and purposelessness that had already set in. Once again, she was no longer a daughter, or a wife, or anything. She was a mother only in name. She hadn't seen Stewart or Molly in weeks; she'd smelled their pillows when they were not at home, but she hadn't been able to face them. She was a hardware-store owner, an uncaught criminal, and a friend of the strange woman across the street, one that grew poisonous plants to boot.

"Now, you must decide what to do with the keys. We both know that you can't keep them."

"I wouldn't want to," she paused, "but I think I have an idea."

Euphemia looked at Lou as though trying to decide whether or not she could trust her, but they'd gotten this far together; that trust must have been earned.

"What's your plan?"

"You'll find out soon enough."

False Spring

CHAPTER 23

Lou cut the packing tape on one of her boxes with an X-Acto Knife. The sun was setting, and her back ached from lifting and rearranging boxes and furniture all day, but she liked the physical finality of being fully settled in one place even if her possessions were still in cardboard boxes. She'd packed haphazardly enough that she had not known what she would find inside each box. She'd discovered books packed between teacups, photo albums, and obituary clippings from over the years, jammed in with sheet music and sketchbooks. As she tore the tape from a box, she paused and looked up to see her belongings strewn across the floor of her parents' house. *Her* house. The house where she'd lived happily as a child and would live happily in her new life.

Opening the flaps of a box, she found a small gold frame with a photo of her parents, her own wedding album, and her box of ticket stubs, movie tickets, library receipts, and paper ephemera that she'd collected over the years. Magician slept on a yellow cushion by the fireplace.

She hadn't felt this light in months.

After moving from the hardware store, her separation felt more permanent. Edward had begrudgingly helped her pack, but they agreed Lou was going to remain in town and run the store with Cass' help until she left for university. The children could stay at either house whenever they wanted, and they would respect one another's space and privacy. She was forging ahead and creating a new path for herself that had nothing to do with anyone else.

Lou had entrusted Cass with a set of keys to the store so that she could take opening and closing shifts. When Louise had last seen her, Cass was putting varnish on pieces of oak, and the glinting focus in her eyes reminded her of her mother when she latched onto a new project. The housekeys were dealt with, the only people that knew what she'd done wouldn't dare speak, she'd invited Euphemia over for tea as her first guest, and her children were coming to stay with her the following night.

All was well.

Lou was unconcerned as to how she would fill the house—she had a cat, she might get another, and her parents' possessions were still strewn around as though they'd never left. She would fill the uninhabited rooms with bookshelves and candles and armchairs she'd hunt down at garage sales.

She simply knew that she was in the right place.

Lou had brought the old record player home from the store and set it up with a Stevie Nicks album. She was about to roll the packing tape into a ball and try to throw it into the garbage bin across the room when the doorbell rang. Through the peephole, Lou saw Bart Hastings and Indigo Higgins with bottles of wine in hand. Lou opened the door, and they were in her entryway before she could say *hello, what are you doing here?* She didn't get to ask the question, but it must have shown on her face.

"We heard you were moving back into the old house. We wanted to stop in and say welcome home!" They pushed the bottles of wine toward her, and once her hands were full, Lou could only point at where they should put their coats and bags. Her parents' old entryway bench was covered in dust, but they didn't seem to mind getting their coats dirty.

"What a nice surprise," Lou said since she hadn't expected company of any kind on her first night back in the house. "Make yourselves at home." She figured this was as much a curiosity experiment of theirs as it was a housewarming.

"Do you need any help unpacking?" they asked.

"I'm all right! Just make yourselves comfortable."

The doorbell rang again, and she let Phillip into the house with his metal detector. Before the evening was over, Lou had opened the door fifteen times for various townsfolk who wanted to welcome her home. In between opening the door for guests, she tried to mitigate the damage the guests could do to her belongings. They'd taken it upon themselves to help her unpack. She imagined there were certain items she would never see again. It would be like the carrot and the wedding ring; she would go to open a drawer and find something completely unexpected, and then would remember the first night in her house.

When Cass arrived, she carried a box in front of her that was large enough to hold a globe. Lou knew what would be inside.

"Come on in," Lou said taking the box from Cass' arms, "everyone else is already here."

Euphemia was the last to arrive in her red coat, with a paper bag at her side and yet another bottle of white wine cradled in her arm. Lou opened the door and wrapped her arms around Euphemia, who stiffened at first, and then settled into the hug, which Lou suddenly realized, was their first.

When they returned to the living room, Frank said, "We couldn't let one of our own move into a new house without a celebration of some kind." He looked less pale than the last time Lou had seen him, and when he looked over at Euphemia, Lou saw her wink at him.

Frank unwrapped brown packing paper to display kitchen glasses, which he decided to place on the mantel. Bart attempted to tackle her books and seemed to be working through some kind of organizational system that Lou couldn't understand. It certainly wasn't alphabetical or by colour. When Lou saw him take a copy of his own book out of the banker's box, he smiled at the cover, gave the book a sniff, and put it on the top shelf. Indigo opened one of the few boxes that didn't have a location scrawled in sharpie across the top; it was the box that Cass had arrived with. Indigo gasped as she opened the flaps and pulled out a spherical sculpture made of keys. The bow of each key had been welded to the tip of another so that each key had a companion above, below, and on either side until the keys formed a perfect sphere with no rough edges, no beginning or endings, no seams. Lou had spent an entire evening soldering with Cass and her hands still smelled metallic if she brought them to her face.

"What a perfectly marvelous sculpture. Where did you get it?" Indigo asked. The others came from their corners of the room to see and feel the key sphere for themselves.

"Cass helped me make it," Lou said. Now, everyone in the room was listening.

"Are these keys *all yours*?" Indigo asked.

"Not exactly, but—"

"How many places have you lived?" Bart had taken the copy of his own book down from the shelf and held under his arm as though he might try to smuggle it from Lou's collection.

"I just picked them up here and there, you know. A few of them are old housekeys of mine. I was in the mood for a new project." She looked over at Cass first, who smiled with pride at a job well done, then at Euphemia, who nodded and tipped her glass as though saying *cheers*. Indigo passed the ball to Frank, and Lou could tell he was resisting the temptation to throw it like a beachball. But even if he did, she knew the keys would never separate. Their edges were melted together so that one key ended where another began.

Ever since her father had taught her to use the key cutter, Lou had loved the semantics of keys: the bow, the shoulder, the biting, the tip, the code, the blade. Now, she could look at them every day and have no choice but to remember and resist the temptation to count them and then put them to use.

"Could you make me one of these?" Indigo asked, "It would be marvelous for the bookstore."

Lou stifled a laugh by turning it into a cough into her sleeve. "I don't know," Lou said, "It took me years to collect enough keys to make this."

"I can wait."

*****

By the end of the evening, Lou's belongings were out of their boxes, which sat, flattened, in the entranceway. Nothing was in the right place. Her cutlery was in the tray, but the tray was on the living room end table. Afghans were strewn across the backs of kitchen chairs, the little box with her ephemera was in the entryway, and Bart's system for organizing the books didn't seem to be a system at all. It looked as though he'd organized the books from smallest to largest so that one end of the bookshelf bowed in a U-shape beneath the weight of hardcovers. Someone had ordered a couple of pizzas, and when they arrived, no one admitted to ordering any, so Lou took out her wallet and tipped the driver generously. She placed the pizza boxes in the centre of her parents' dining room table, and they began to eat. Someone had unpacked the kitchenware, but couldn't remember where they had put plates. Lou sectioned paper towels as makeshift plates, and they dug in. The arrangement of guests around the table reminded Lou of Thanksgiving: how Phillip had clattered the turkey tray and spiked the punch, how Euphemia had pointed out crows sitting outside the windows, how Lou had asked for a divorce. And how she'd been comforted by Euphemia. It had only been a few months, but it felt like a decade had passed. Lou felt older, but not in a bad way. She wanted to resist the cliché, but she felt more perceptive. She knew more about these people than she'd ever wanted to, and she enjoyed the weight of that knowledge.

Their secrets were safe with her. She no longer felt undone; she was home.

After the majority of her guests had left, the only ones left were Euphemia and Phillip, but he'd drunk slightly too much of the wine everyone had so generously brought and decided to take a nap in Lou's freshly made bed. She wasn't sure he would ever leave, but she had plenty of extra space and nothing to hide. Not anymore.

Lou had watched Indigo unwrapping wine glasses by the closet. Sure enough, she found two glasses still wrapped in brown packing paper on the shoe rack and washed them in the sink before pouring a substantial amount of wine into each. With full glasses of wine, Lou and Euphemia sat on the living room couch among the detritus of her move. The key sculpture was in the centre of the coffee table.

"How does it feel to be back here?" Euphemia asked.

"After everything that's happened, I never imagined I'd be moving back into this house." Sensing that there was more, Euphemia said nothing, and waited for Lou to continue. "You knew my parents, Euphemia. You must have known if something was wrong." Lou sipped her wine and waited for the answer to the question she'd been waiting to ask for months. "*Did* you know?"

Euphemia took a moment before she began. She looked at Lou, the woman she'd blackmailed, who had since become her closest friend, and she decided to speak. "I may not know absolutely everything that happens in this town, but I think I would have known if your parents had planned a suicide. It was an accident, a horrible one, but it *was* an accident. You shouldn't blame yourself, Louise."

It felt right to hear these words in her old house, that had been their house. For the first time since their deaths, Louise felt certain that it had all been an accident.

"I won't blame myself," she said so softly that it sounded like a mantra—something she said only for herself. It was an accident. They had made a mistake. They hadn't planned to die. She'd been right all along.

She knew that Euphemia was the keeper of secrets, her accomplice, and her co-conspirator. Lou could live in this house and remember the years spent here without blaming herself. She would continue to grieve, and she expected to grieve for the rest of her life, but she could grieve in peace.

Even so, she could hear the words that Euphemia didn't say: she couldn't possibly know what Lou's parents had been thinking or whether they had left the car running intentionally. In all of her years in Snowton, she'd learned that it was never useful to speculate about what someone was thinking. Euphemia had an unrivalled sense of intuition and an uncanny ability to spin a good story. Lou was sure that she didn't see any harm in bringing her friend some peace, even if she couldn't be certain of what had happened.

Phillip continued to snore in the next room, and after an hour or so, Euphemia poured the remainder of the wine into her glass and Lou's, and then reached into the paper bag at her feet. Inside was a small potted lavender plant.

"A housewarming gift. Not poisonous—just calming and fragrant."

Lou leaned towards the plant and breathed in the scent of lavender. It made the room smell calm, like there was life in it again, even if it was small and rooted in one place.

"I'm afraid I must be off," Euphemia said as she lifted herself from the couch cushions. "I need to pay a visit to an old friend who owes me a favor."

"Who would that be?"

"Frank Blake. He's going to paint my fence."

"I'm not sure that's such a good idea, he was pretty drunk when he left here."

"I'll give him a couple of hours to sleep it off and then put him to work bright and early."

"What was the promise he made you?"

"Oh *that*. I forgot to tell you. He's going to take Isabella's money and open a town museum. It's time we shared some history in Snowton." Euphemia chuckled as Lou handed over her coat, said goodbye, and shut the door behind her.

Alone again, Lou arranged the rest of her belongings around the house and cleared a place for the plant on the fireplace mantle between the gold-framed photo of her parents and a photo of Stewart and Molly. She had a hunch about this particular plant, but she hadn't wanted to test her theory with Euphemia in the room. She dug her fingers in the moistened earth until she found what she was looking for. Between the dirt and the roots of the lavender plant were the sharp and familiar edges of Euphemia's housekey.

Acknowledgements

We talk about writing as a solitary endeavour, but this novella would not exist without some key people.

Thank you so much to my family who has always supported my writing: thank you to my mother for being my first editor, to my father for building me a writing desk out of maple (and for woodworking knowledge), to Katie and Aideen for being cheerleaders at every turn.

Thank you to the 2016 "100 pages in 100 days" cohort for providing input into the very first iteration of this story, when it was about a man named Ed. I hope you read it and see that I took your advice; I do listen!

To my beta readers: Adrienne Adams, Alex Allen, Daniel Cowper, Sue Hirst, Eden Middleton, Heather Robertson, Mallory Smith, and Brandon Teigland, thank you so much for spending your valuable time reading messy and incomplete drafts. I'm proud to call such talented and generous people my friends.

Thank you to everyone on Twitter who responded when I asked, "What is the most horrifying thing you could find inside a garden gnome?" Your answers did not disappoint and will haunt my nightmares for years to come.

Thank you to the graduate student community at the University of Calgary. You inspire me every day to work harder and be kinder. Thank you to the wider creative writing community in Calgary: the crews at *filling Station*, *NōD Magazine*, Loft 112, Shelf Life Books, Pages, and the Writers' Guild of Alberta.

Thank you to so many friends who have listened to me talk about this book for the past four years and provided encouragement, coffee dates, distraction, trips to the mountains, strange articles about key cutting, and so much more. You know who you are, and I am grateful to have you in my life.

Thank you to Naomi K. Lewis for your keen eye and sharp edits.

Finally, thank you to Aritha van Herk who always reminds me to trust myself. You have been a mentor to me in more than just the mechanics of writing, and I am forever grateful for your guidance.

*****

Notes:

The epigraph to this book is Robert Kroestch's poem "Keyed In" from *Too Bad: Sketches Toward a Self Portrait*, University of Alberta Press, 2010. Reprinted with permission.

Three quotations in this book are taken from other sources:

On page 3, the phrase Lou hears in the cemetery is from Louisa May Alcott.
On page 8, the quotation on Lou's father's headstone is from Charles Dickens.
On page 24, the italicized quotation is from Vladimir Nabokov.

Photo by David Kang

AMY LEBLANC is a writer and editor based in Calgary, Alberta. She is a recipient of the Lieutenant Governor of Alberta Emerging Artist Award and author of the poetry collection *I know something you don't know.*

BRAVE & BRILLIANT SERIES

SERIES EDITOR:
Aritha van Herk, Professor, English, University of Calgary
ISSN 2371-7238 (PRINT) ISSN 2371-7246 (ONLINE)

Brave & Brilliant encompasses fiction, poetry, and everything in between and beyond. Bold and lively, each with its own strong and unique voice, Brave & Brilliant books entertain and engage readers with fresh and energetic approaches to storytelling and verse.